WA 1294757 1

KT-451-948

Imogen Rhia Herrad

The Woman who Loved an Octopus
and Other Saints' Tales

IMOGEN Rhia HERRAD

The WOMAN who LOVED AN Octopus
AND OTHER Saints' Tales

seren

Seren is the book imprint of
Poetry Wales Press Ltd
57 Nolton Street, Bridgend, Wales CF31 3AE
www.seren-books.com

© Imogen Rhia Herrad, 2007

ISBN 978-1-85411-442-6

The right of Imogen Rhia Herrad to be identified as the author of
this work has been asserted in accordance with the Copyright,
Designs and Patents Act, 1988.

A CIP record for this title is available from
the British Library.

All rights reserved. No part of this publication
may be reproduced, stored in a retrieval system,
or transmitted at any time or by any means
electronic, mechanical, photocopying, recording
or otherwise without the prior permission
of the copyright holder.

Cover illustration and design: Andy Dark

The publisher works with the financial assistance of the
Welsh Books Council.

Printed in Plantin by Creative Print and Design, Wales

Learning Resources
Centre

12947571

Contents

Cofen

Sixth century

Also known as Govan or Goven. St Govan is best known for the chapel wedged between rocks by the sea in which the saint is supposed to have lived as a hermit in the sixth century. When pirates attacked, Govan hid inside a rock that miraculously closed around the saint, opening up again only when the danger had passed.

In fact the famous chapel was only built in the thirteenth century, as far away from St Govan's time as our own. But the altar and a seat cut into the rock are much older and may well date back to the sixth century. Even older was the healing well which used to rise near the chapel, providing fresh water.

Commonly St Govan is assumed to be a man. But there is a story that the person who lived by the sea, tending the holy well, was a woman named Cofen, and maybe no saint at all.

The sea is still and grey and green. A breeze strokes my skin and moves on. The sky has covered its face with clouds. I'm cold.

This is where we first met. I'd never been to this place before. I needed to get away from the city and the people and the chemicals in the air. I needed to breathe.

So I drove to the sea. I parked the car somewhere and clambered down the rocks until I stood on the shingle and breathed salt and seaweed and sand and freedom. There were mermaids singing far out in the water, and the wind put on a dress of whirling sand and danced with me.

The tide came in. I sat on the sand near the water and breathed with the waves, in and out, in and out.

The mermaids' song became wilder the higher the tide rose. And then suddenly there was someone else. There was a bluegreengrey shape in the water, a shimmering and glistening shape with many arms and the deepest eyes in the world. She was watching me. She was there in the water, watching me sitting on the shore.

She was sinuous and sensuous. Her skin shimmered dragonfly blue, aquamarine, pebble grey. She pulsed like a sea anemone. Serpentine arms rose and fell with the breathing of the waves. Her soft tentacles arched. They beckoned to me. My skin shivered with longing for her touch.

She moved closer.

I jumped up and ran away.

I didn't go near the sea for weeks.

I dreamed of it every night. I dreamed of water sparkling silver with sunlight, of pebbles smooth and green and slippery with algae. I dreamed of seaweed streaming like long hair in the current and warm, wet tentacles; softer than water.

Every morning I woke up with the taste of salt on my lips.

I tried to stop it, but the waters rose and rose and there was nothing I could do to resist them.

In the end I gave in and went back to the beach. I parked the car in the same place and clambered down the rocks and dared the sea to come and get me. I resented its pull. I had never felt anything like it. I had always been my own person, from the first moment of my life. I never had a mother. I wasn't born like other people. I hatched out of an egg.

'Come and get me then,' I said to the sea. Far out, there was a bluegreengrey shimmer on the water, like sunlight. But it was a dull day.

The water rose. The tide was coming in. It rose and rose and rose. The waves climbed up the beach, over the sand, over the shingle. I trembled with anticipation. Water touched my shoes, flooded over my feet, climbed up my thighs. Something that felt like a warm, wet finger stroked my leg. Then another. And another. Eight soft bluegreengrey tentacles wandered over me, exploring, touching, stroking.

She tasted of salt like the sea.

Like the sea, she hollowed out my defences. I should have known. The sea reduces cliffs to sand. What chance did I have?

I had a mermaid for a mother. She loved me, but she loved the sea more. One morning I woke up and she was gone. I waited and waited and waited, but she never came back. In the end I gave up and crawled into an egg and stayed there for a long time until somebody put a broody hen on it to see what would happen.

I was captured in the eight arms of my lover. Her beauty captivated me. She taught me how to breathe under water. She didn't need to, every kiss she gave me was a kiss of life.

Together we explored the ocean. Being with her felt like flying. I forgot about air and land and solid ground. I lost my taste for fresh water and became a creature of the sea. We feasted with sharks and dived down to the very bottom of the sea where the kraken lives. Every night, we slept on sand as soft and white as linen sheets. She braided shells and corals into my hair. She found a way into my heart and I didn't know how to get her out of it.

So I left the sea.

But it's not so easy to rid myself of her. She put a spell on me so that I cannot forget her, although I have tried every way I can think of.

I had an ogress for a mother. She had wanted me to be an ogress too because she hated people. She wanted me to come with her when she went to kill and eat them. But I wasn't an ogress and I wasn't like her although I tried and tried. She went away to look for another daughter. I waited and waited and waited, but she never came back.

It's cold by the water. The sky has covered its face with clouds. The sea is still and grey and green.

I come here every day to teach her to leave me alone. I will not go back into the water. I will stare her down when she comes too close to show her that there is no feeling left.

The pebbles on the beach look like eggs, smooth, oval. An egg is like a world of its own. Self-contained. No way in, no way out. Perfect. To achieve contact, you have to break the shell and destroy it. There is no other way.

Nobody is going to break me.

The mermaids are singing again, far out in the bay. I don't want to hear them. I push my hands over my ears and scream at them to shut up and go away. There is a bluegreengrey shimmer in the water. It's only the sun, but I scream at that too.

I want the whole world to go away and leave me alone.

A blue tentacle is stroking my heart and I can't breathe.

I had a soldier for a mother. She was fierce and brave and killed many people in the war. Killing was her job. It was all she could do. When she came back home from the war, she took her gun and she killed me. I waited and waited, but she didn't kill herself to be with me.

It's raining. I sit in the shelter I have built for myself and watch the rain hit the sea. The tide is coming in, but it can't come as far as where I'm sitting. I made sure of that. I won't be captured again. I will sit here out of reach until she's learned that she can't get me. Then I will leave and not sooner. I don't want her to forget me. I want her to know that she can't have me.

The waves come creeping nearer. And nearer. The waters rise and rise. A bluegreen shimmer beckons.

I turn myself into a rock. I look on, unmoved as stone, as she tries and tries to get near me. Nobody gets near me.

And when the tide turns at last and the water recedes, I hurl all the rocks and pebbles I can after it to make it stay away. I want to build a dam around me to keep the water out forever.

But a stone is stuck in my throat and I can't breathe.

I will not cry. I will not cry. I beat my hands on the rocks until they bleed. That will give you something to cry for.

I had a bitch for a mother. She was nice some days and on others beat me black and blue. She shut me in a cupboard for days without food. Pembroke Social Services have a file on her but it wasn't enough to take me away from her although I begged to be taken away. When she heard about that, she was devastated that I did not want to stay with her, and I felt terribly guilty. I did not know how to keep her out of my heart.

She is still alive. She lives in a rest home and people think she's a nice old lady.

I turn my back on the sea and walk inland. I walk and walk and walk until I'm tired enough to drop, but not tired enough to sleep. Whichever way I turn, I'm going towards the beach. There are webs between my fingers and I can't unlock the door of my car when I finally find it.

The waves call my name and the mermaids are singing. Their voices follow me, travelling on the wind.

A green tentacle strokes my heart.

I clamber down the rocks until I stand on the shingle and breathe salt and seaweed and memory. The water has risen higher than my shelter. She comes gliding towards me, walking on the water.

She is sinuous and sensuous. Her skin shimmers dragonfly blue, aquamarine, pebble grey. She pulses like a sea anemone. My skin shivers with longing for her touch.

I swim towards her.

# Madryn

Fifth century

Madryn or Madrun was the granddaughter of Gwrtheyrn (or Vortigern),
the British king who invited the Saxons
into Britain to help fight off the Picts and
other sea raiders. When it turned out that
the Saxons were a bigger threat by far, his
own people turned against Gwrtheyrn
and he had to flee with his family.
Madryn, her baby son Ceidio, and her
grandfather sought refuge in a wooden
fort on the Llyn Peninsula, which was set
alight. Gwrtheyrn died in the fire.
Madryn managed to get away with the
child in her arms, and fled from the
troubles in Wales to another country.

The sky is red. Somebody fires a shot in the street. I spin around, drop the shopping bags I am carrying, crouch down for shelter, try to locate the sniper. People turn and stare, somebody laughs.

The doctor says there is no shooting here, she says it is a car backfiring, fireworks, nothing to worry about.

How does she know? I ask her. How does she know? There was a man shot in this city last week, a girl in the hospital told me about it, she read me an article from her newspaper. People are being shot dead in your city, I tell the doctor. How do you know nobody will be shooting at me?

Because we are not at war, she says. You are not in the war anymore. Sometimes people get shot, yes, but it is rare. It does not happen often.

But it does, I say.

Not often, she says. You are safe here.

I say nothing. I look out of the window of her room. There is a little bit of grey sky with birds in it, and black roof tops. In her window, the sky is grey. In this room, where I come twice a week to talk, I am almost safe, for a while. This room is in the doctor's world where people are safe, where the sky is grey, where there are no shots, only fireworks.

I would feel safer if I still had a weapon, I tell her. I fought at home when we were invaded, right up to the birth I fought. I was a good fighter. People were afraid of me. I was somebody then. I was the king's granddaughter, and a fighter in the field. I was strong and proud. I had my weapons, and even though there was war and fighting and killing, I felt safer then than I do now.

Weapons kill, she says.

Yes, I say. I feel naked without a weapon. Skinless.

Then I say nothing and look out of her window again, and there is a new silence in the room.

ᴀ ᴀ ᴀ

How is your baby? the doctor asks.
Still in the hospital, I say, which she knows. Recovering, I say, which means nothing.
I don't say: I have a baby with bandages for a body. Bandages for a face. No mouth, no nose, no eyes.
I don't say: They're going to try another skin graft next week but they don't know if it'll work this time.
How is your baby? the doctor asks, and I flinch. The question sounds like an accusation.

ᴀ ᴀ ᴀ

When I was first taken to this room to talk I expected somebody who would want answers from me.
I wondered what I should do. To say nothing is dangerous. When you say nothing, it means that you will not co-operate.
To say too much is dangerous. People will become suspicious if you talk too willingly.
I was surprised that the questioner was a woman. The other doctor had only told me that he thought it would help me to see a specialist. A therapist. He said the word slowly and looked at me, drawing breath to explain to me what a therapist does. I should have let him. It might even have been amusing to listen to him talking in terms he thought suitable for me, the refugee from a primitive, war-torn country: soul doctor and bad spirits that needed driving out of my troubled self.
A therapist, I said. Ah well. I would have preferred a Jungian analyst. Still, we can't have all we want, can we?
That shut him up. Later though I wished I hadn't said it. To speak without thinking means you have less control over what

you say. Now they know that I know about therapy and analysis, that I might be able to see through some of their simpler tricks. I have given myself away. They will have to use the big guns now and I might not be able to withstand those.

When it was time for the first session, I forgot about my decision to appear to allow myself to be drawn out, to talk, apparently reluctantly, slowly, but to talk. I just sat and looked at her. I listened to what she said, not to her words, but trying to find the sense behind them. I wanted to sniff out her intentions, tried to work out what it really was she wanted to find out.

ᐃ ᐃ ᐃ

She rarely asks questions. More often, she will just sit and look at me, or out of her window, or to a point just to the side of me. At first I worried that she was giving a signal to somebody. But behind me is nothing but a blank wall.

I am trying to understand why you are so afraid, she says.

I don't like her asking questions. I am trying to understand you means I am trying to look inside your head so that I will know which levers to pull.

I decide to challenge her. Why? I ask back.

She wrinkles her forehead, appearing to give my question thought.

Because I feel that there is something in the way, she says. We seem to be running on the spot without getting anywhere.

I am pleased to hear this. I have been successful in resisting her, but she doesn't seem to have noticed that I'm doing it on purpose. She thinks it's because I'm afraid.

Unless it's a trick. It might well be a trick, lulling me into believing she is worried, into believing I have tricked her when she sees through me perfectly well.

Why do you think I'm afraid? I ask.

She leans forward over her desk, looks at me earnestly. She had wanted me to sit in a corner of her office, on the sofa or an

armchair, and she would have sat in the other armchair. She
said it would be more relaxed. But I said I preferred her sitting
at her desk. I said it was more professional, but the truth is that
I prefer to have the desk between her and me. It gives me a
small advantage in case I have to run away.

You have been through terrible things, she says. The
invasion, the war, your grandfather dying, your baby wounded
in the fire.

I hate being reminded, having my nose rubbed in my
infirmities, my misfortunes.

So, she says, I would expect you to be traumatised, of course.

I hate being told that I conform to her expectations. Why
does she need me to tell her anything at all if she knows everything about me anyway?

In fact, she says, you have come through this remarkably
well. You managed to save yourself and your son.

That means: you're not that badly traumatised, you don't
warrant all that much help and sympathy. You can look after
yourself after all. You're tough.

But, she says, there appears to be something more specific.
There is something sharply defined that you appear to be terri-
fied of. I would expect you to be hypersensitised generally,
which you are. But there is something more than that. At least
that is my impression.

She leans back again. This, she explained to me at the
beginning, is so as not to crowd my space.

I prefer it when she shows emotion, because then I can read
her more easily.

What do you think there might be? I ask her. It might give
me an idea of what she thinks.

I don't know, she says. Only you can tell me.

Why should I, I say, my voice flat. I hadn't meant to say
that, certainly not in the way it came out, as hostile as that.

She says nothing. She is good at saying nothing.

To break this silence would be to give up, to give in, to wave the white flag and signal surrender. I would have to trust her blindly, put my fate, my past and my future, into her hands.

I say nothing.

She says nothing.

I think of another room, another questioner, another me.

⁂

I want to scream at the doctor. You don't understand at all, I want to scream. You have no idea. No idea. You think the world is safe. You have never been in a war. You don't understand. The fact that I can sit here and not tell you anything means I trust you enough to believe that you're not going to have me punished for not co-operating.

But I would rather cut off my thumbs than tell her that.

⁂

The sky is red. In my dream, I am running, stumbling, my lungs burning with smoke. I know that I am dreaming but it makes no difference. The night it happened, I kept telling myself that it was all a nightmare. I ran away from the fire with the screaming baby and told myself, this is not really happening, it is only a dream. But it wasn't. It was real and it never ended. It still goes on, and my dreams are more real now than my waking hours in this grey country where people tell me that life is safe. I can hear the baby's screams. They pierce my ears like an electric drill.

After I was captured, I saw an electric drill being put through a man's hands. I heard his shrieks even over the screaming of the drill. He wasn't killed. It wouldn't have been so bad if he had been. It would have been over. But he wasn't killed.

I had to sit next to the man in the interrogation room and watch. When I tried to close my eyes they hit me, and then they hit the man. I had to watch. I kept my eyes fixed on the drill, I studied the drill until I could have drawn it with my eyes closed. It was dark green and orange and on the side of it were the words Made in Germany, and while I sat there, a part of my mind detached itself from that room and made plans for how I would get away, and swore that I would never go to that country Germany, never, never, no matter what. And that's why, when I finally got away, I didn't stop there although the other refugees said it was a good place, with good medical care for my son, and that I should stay. But I couldn't stay. I went on, north and west until I came to the Channel, and the train and London. I know it's arbitrary. It could have said Made in Britain on the drill and I'd be in Munich or Berlin now instead. I don't expect anybody would accept it as a reason, even if I told them, and I won't. But that's why I'm here, because I had to watch an electric drill put through a man's hands.

After they had finished with the man they said they would start on the baby. They had someone carry my son in, and a man stood over him with the drill that was still smeared with blood from the other prisoner, and they said it was either the drill in my son's belly or I would talk and tell them the truth. They said they were tired of my games.

They started the drill.

∆ ∆ ∆

I killed my grandfather, I tell the doctor. I watch her face. I want to see if she will understand.

She watches me back. I can see what she's thinking: Patient blames herself for grandfather's death. Survivor's guilt.

I say nothing.

She says nothing.

Finally she asks, how did you kill him?

My mouth opens and I say, I pushed him. I pushed him and he stumbled and he fell into the fire. That's how I killed him.

And then I say nothing at all after that. I have made sure that she won't believe me when I tell her what really happened.

ᐞ ᐞ ᐞ

How is your baby? the doctor asks.

Another operation yesterday, I say. The skin of my face feels like paper. My eyes burn. I was up all night, sitting by the bandages and tubes and beeping machines that are as close as I can get to my son. The nurses didn't send me away. They only said that the operation had gone better than they'd dared hope, and that they would keep him sedated for a while longer, and not to be disappointed if he didn't come round. I think what they meant was that there was no point in me staying, but I stayed anyway, and they didn't send me away.

Maybe the last operation, I say.

But I'm too tired to hope. I'm too afraid to hope. I don't tell her that.

But when she smiles and says, I'm glad for you, that's really good news; I don't contradict her.

ᐞ ᐞ ᐞ

No, I said. I had to scream it over the noise the drill made. No no no please no please please.

They switched the drill off. Looked at me.

So the bitch has decided to talk, has she? Maybe she has a heart after all.

I'll tell you what you want, I said. My eyes burned. The inside of my mouth felt like paper. I wanted to say: I will tell you nothing, I will not betray the things I believe in, the people I care about. But instead I said: I'll tell you what you want. Everything. Only don't hurt my child.

I betrayed my grandfather in exchange for the life of my son.

I told the men in the interrogation room about the place where my grandfather was hiding, and how to get inside. I hoped the password had been changed in the time since my capture.

They were gone three days.

They tied me up and left me alone in my dark cell, no food, no water. I could only just feed the baby. I couldn't clean him, or myself. I couldn't stop him screaming. I was terribly afraid that the men had left, that the baby would starve, that I would starve, alone in the dark.

I thought of my grandfather. The last time I'd seen him we'd quarrelled. I had seen the whole mess coming. I'd even told him that if he thought getting in one lot of bandits to fight another was a smart idea, then he was probably more senile than he appeared and it was time to hand over the reins of power to someone else. He said the only reason he wasn't going to throw me out was that my son might one day follow my father or him on the throne. I told him he could keep his throne. But he hadn't been able to. The *coup* happened two days later, and we'd been on the run since then.

I prayed that the men wouldn't find him.

They came back after three days, stinking of smoke, and told me what they had done. They told me that they had beaten my grandfather and lit the building around him. They told me how he had cursed me with his dying breath, in the flames.

Then they poured petrol over everything and set fire to the prison too, and then they left.

I don't know how I got out. All I can remember thinking is that I had sacrificed my grandfather for the life of my son, and that the sacrifice must not have been for nothing. If the baby died, my betrayal would have been for nothing.

I never told anybody. When I got to London and claimed asylum and they asked me what had happened, I said that my grandfather had died in the fire and that I ran away with the baby.

Now I owe my grandfather a life. I owe my him my son's life.

In my dreams under the red sky, my grandfather comes tottering, a human torch, faceless, his hands stretched out like claws. I know what he wants. He wants my son's life. That's why I have to watch the baby as he sleeps, because I am afraid my grandfather's spirit is going to come and take him.

ᴀ ᴀ ᴀ

I killed my grandfather, I tell the doctor.

She watches my face. I think she tries to understand.

I say nothing.

She says nothing.

Finally she asks, do you want to tell me how you killed him?

With words, I say.

I tell her how.

And now he will...

I hadn't meant to say that.

And now he will? she asks

I look at her. He will come back and fetch my son, I say. A life for a life.

Is that what you were so afraid of? she asks.

I say nothing.

He won't come back, she says. Your grandfather is dead because he was killed by war criminals. You are traumatised, and your little boy is in hospital, because you were tortured and nearly killed by the same war criminals. Your grandfather's ghost won't come back to steal your little boy's soul. Can you believe that? Can you try?

I look back at her.

I don't say no.

nnon

Fifth century

anhun [m] – (n) sleeplessness
Annon, or Anhun, was the handmaid of
Queen Madryn of Gwent (herself a
saint). It is said that, together with her
mistress, Annon founded a church at
Trawsfynydd.

She and Queen Madryn were return-
ing from a pilgrimage to Bardsey Island
when night fell and they stopped at the
place that is today the town of
Trawsfynydd. There they both had the
same dream in which they heard a voice
telling them: *'Adeiladwch eglwys yma'* –
'Build a church here'.

I'd like to be able to say that she came in the night, like a thief, to steal me away. In fact she arrived on the boat from Pwllheli like everybody else. I saw her get off as it lay moored in the island harbour on Saturday morning.

I wasn't actually at the harbour when the boat came in. I do not mix much with people. They call me the Hermit Nun, although I am not a nun. I don't belong to any order.

I am on a retreat. I'm retreating from the world and its people. I try to live close to God's creation; air and sea and silence and the huge blue question mark of the sky.

Most of the visitors who come for the week only don't even know that I am here. Some may catch a glimpse of me on my way to chapel early mornings or evenings, and ask who I am. But I never talk to them. I never talk to anybody. I keep my distance, my silence.

When the boat came into the harbour that morning I was standing on a little hill that overlooks the sea and the harbour.

I saw the boat come in around the side of the mountain, nosing past the rocks where seals will lie sunning themselves at low tide. There was a little knot of departing visitors at the landing stage; and some of the people who spend all summer on the island, come to look at the fresh intake of weekly visitors.

And there they were, clambering off the rocking boat onto the landing stage, one after the other. There she was, although I didn't know her then. I just saw a middle-aged woman, short and thick-set, wearing brightly coloured clothes. One of the visitors. They'd all be gone soon enough, and another lot would come next Saturday to replace them.

Few of them stay longer than the week. The silence and the emptiness get to them, the absence of amusements, electricity, television. There is nothing here to take your mind off things. You find that very soon your self and your life loom large, echoing like sound in a cathedral because nothing gets in the way. There is nothing else here.

You are alone with God.

It is a chance but most see it as a threat. So much emptiness, they say, looking at the sky full of blues and greys and clouds and birds, at the endlessness of the sea and all the shades of green and grey of the island. So much emptiness they say; looking, not seeing.

They fill up the silence with their noise, with the things they bring to remind them of home. They find me unnatural, think it uncanny that I don't talk. They do not understand that it is only by avoiding the noise of their lives, their voices, that I can strain to hear the voice of God.

Don't misunderstand me – there is no big voice booming down from heaven, no miracle shafts of light, no seagulls speaking in tongues. But to hear the voice of God in prayer, there needs to be silence; a silence of the spirit as well as an absence of noise. I empty myself to be ready for God.

'Is that your sister who arrived yesterday?' the shepherd asked when I met him early next morning on my way back from chapel.

I looked at him, not understanding.

'One of the new lot. She got here on the boat yesterday morning. You must have seen her. She's the spitting image of you.'

I shook my head. Frowned. I do not have a sister. As far as I could remember there had not been anybody on the boat who looked like me.

'Ah, well,' he said, moving on. 'You'll meet her sometime, I expect. Can see for yourself then.'

I nodded good morning and walked on up the mountain to

the Saint's cave. A millennium and a half ago, it was home to a holy man. He lived on this island, existing on water and the fish that God sent for his food. I sat down by the cave entrance, closing my eyes; hands folded in my lap to keep them still.

I do not see visions when I pray. I'm not given to visions.

I hear.

I listen, and I hear.

This is the music of the spheres: a great rushing and humming, black and silver and blue, greater than anything we can imagine.

I prayed, and I listened, and I was filled with joy.

'There she is,' the shepherd said the next morning. It was very early, the air sharp and cold, not long after sunrise, the grass still wet with dew. I was on my way to chapel. He whistled to his dog, then moved his head to indicate a figure walking towards the chapel. 'Another believer, by the look of it. You're going to meet her now. I would have thought it was you, if it hadn't been for the clothes!'

I looked.

There was a woman; not young, and stockily built, her grey hair pulled back into a plait. She wore a long skirt of brightly coloured material, red and orange and purple; some ethnic jacket. She walked, head bowed, with measured strides. The thought came to me that she was trying to look like her idea of a devout person.

Another believer, indeed. A tree-hugger, more likely.

I gave her a nod when I entered the chapel, and was relieved when she just returned my greeting without attempting to talk.

'I hear you're spending all summer here,' she said after the service, when we were walking away from the chapel. Her earrings jingled as she walked.

I nodded.

'I'd love to go on a real retreat.' Her voice sounded wistful.

'I went for a week last year, a Buddhist retreat near St David's; only a week is not the same, is it? I just haven't got the time. Or the money.'

'Then make time,' I said, breaking my silence. 'For God. What could be more important?'

'The Goddess is in all of us,' she replied. It sounded like something she had learnt by heart. 'Twenty-four hours a day, seven days a week. She is there for us.'

I said nothing.

She sighed. 'And some of us have to earn a living.'

I inclined my head; the gesture saying as well as any words could, that the birds of the air neither sow nor reap, and yet God feeds them.

We arrived at the fork in the road. I gave her a nod and went on my way, towards the house for breakfast and then the mountain and the hermit's cave.

The sky arched over the island, its brilliance singing in my eyes. The sunlight dazzled me. I took a breath and tasted beauty on my tongue. I was wrapped in the blue of the Virgin's mantle. Even when I closed my eyes I saw nothing but blue. I gave praise to God. I closed my eyes and I opened my ears, and I prayed.

I prayed, and I listened. But my ears were not opened. I sat and I prayed and I felt like a vessel stoppered up, so that nothing will go in and nothing come out. I sat with my eyes closed and my hands folded in my lap, and I called upon God to open up my ears, but He did not answer. I sat and I prayed, and when I opened my eyes the air was flooded with gold and copper and the sky streaked with green and blue and yellow, and it was evening.

A road of light stretched from where I was sitting: it went across the waters of the Sound to the mountains of the mainland, wound itself round the hills. I closed my eyes and opened them again, but not before I had seen two figures walking on the road of light, walking away towards the mainland.

I shook my head like a dog just out of the water.

Now all I could see was the sunset.

There was a chill in the air. I got up. Time for evening service.

She was there again, but this time she did not try to talk to me. We prayed together, and afterwards walked home in silence. She smiled good night as we reached the fork in the road; nodded, and was gone.

The waves breathed in and out, in and out, in and out. I blew out my candle and went to bed.

There was a voice in the dark, and it spoke to me. *Follow the road I have laid down for you.* I stood on a hill overlooking a valley and steeply rising mountains beyond. Ragged grey clouds moved swiftly across the sky. The air was cool and damp. *Build my church here,* the voice said.

With that I woke up. The room was pitch dark. There wasn't a sound except for the whispering of the sea outside.

My ears were ringing with words.

The sky next morning as I walked to chapel was the palest shade of aquamarine. The morning was cold and clear and exquisite.

As soon as she saw me, her eyes became round as marbles and she opened her mouth and drew breath to talk.

I nodded a greeting, sat down and lowered my head in prayer.

After the service, there was no holding her.

'I had the strangest dream last night,' she said. 'I saw the two of us walking away from here together, on to the mainland. And then I heard a voice...' She looked at me. 'Do you ever have... you know, visions?'

I shook my head.

'I do,' she said. 'The Goddess shows me things, sometimes.' She stopped and looked at me. 'She has got plans for us. I'm so glad! I was hoping something would happen. That's why I came here to the island. It's supposed to be a holy place. I was hoping for a miracle.' She gave me a radiant smile. 'And now I've got one.'

All day long I sat on the mountain by the Saint's cave, praying and straining to listen, but in vain. My ears were closed to the music of the spheres.

That night in my dreams, I saw myself being led away; not on a path of light this time, but an ordinary tarmac road in the drizzle. There were hills on both sides and mountains rising before us; and no sign of the sea anywhere.
Follow the road I have laid down for you.
The mountains drew closer together. A valley opened up in front of us.
Build my church here.
I awoke. It was dark.
I got up, pulled on my clothes. I found my torch by touch and let myself out.
The air was dark and cold, the sky brilliant with stars. The chapel windows glowed golden. When I pushed the door open, there was warmth and light. Somebody had lit the candles.
She was kneeling by the altar, head bowed, lost in prayer. She did not look up when I came in and pulled the door closed after me.
I knelt down, attempted to empty my mind of all thought. There was a great rushing in my ears like a waterfall. It was not the music of the spheres. It was the noise made by my fear.
Lord, into Your hands I commend my spirit.

'You saw it too,' she said as we walked away from the chapel after morning service. Her smile shone. Her earrings tinkled.
I raised my eyebrows. Her display of joy struck me as almost unseemly.

'I know you did. Aren't you delighted? I'm so happy.'

I said nothing.

'It was the same as last night, like a dream; but it wasn't a dream. The two of us, walking towards this place in the mountains. It's drizzling and cloudy, and then we come to a valley and the voice says, *Build my temple here.*' She turned to me. 'She's calling us. She has chosen us.'

I broke my silence again, offering up a prayer for forgiveness at the same time. 'Perhaps *He* is calling *you.*'

'Us,' she repeated. 'She, He – it doesn't matter. She's calling you and me.'

'That is absurd,' I said, and added as an afterthought, 'I have renounced the world.'

'You can renounce the world without fleeing from it.'

'I am not fleeing from it. I have come here where it's quiet and far away from most things.' How would she understand? How could I share a vision with this hippie? I never see visions. I am not given to them. 'I feel closer to God here than anywhere else.'

'God – the Goddess.' She tipped her head back, opened her arms wide. The morning sunshine lay on the planes of her face. 'They're only names. You have been led here. By God, you would say. By the Goddess, I would say. By the Creative Spirit who is neither male nor female, who resides in all of us.'

The Spirit. I must subdue my spirit.

'You must follow it,' she said.

No, no, no.

I want to stay here.

Here, where the neversleeping sea is my heavenly bridegroom, where the yellow flames of the gorse speak in tongues in my ear. I have found the garden of Eden, and you want to banish me from it, lead me into a world that is full of serpents.

'We have been chosen!' she declared, almost gloating. I remembered how she had said, yesterday, 'I was hoping for a

36 *Imogen Rhia Herrad*

miracle. And now I've got one.' This was why she'd come here. Blatantly. Going to a holy place looking for a miracle. Taking a short cut. Not preparing herself, waiting in patience and humility until it pleased God to elect her; but pushing, rushing forward until she was in the front row.

Buddhist retreats.

Goddess worship.

A miracle hunter. She probably put her visions on the internet.

The fact that I shun the world does not mean that I am unworldly.

She won't get far, I thought. Then remembered that she had already got exactly where she wanted.

I was exhausted. I felt as though I was fighting her for my life on the island.

I started climbing the mountain. My feet stumbled. I looked down.

I was walking, not on coarse short grass, but on a smooth, black surface. A tarmac road. A great wind came rushing down from the hills, bringing with it land smells of wet earth and leaves and grass.

The wind was humming and sighing and singing in my ears, lifting up my heart.

I do not want to go back into the World.

I felt as though with each step I made, I covered a mile.

The World is full of noise and distraction, destruction and falsehood.

A bird sang from somewhere, hidden in a tree. A dog barked.

I want to stay on this island. Everything I want is here.

I had left the island. I was walking on the road that He had laid down for me. Clouds moved across the sky. I was being propelled towards the mountains at great speed. Fine rain touched the skin of my face, my arms. On the island, I had been walking in hot sunshine.

The mountains drew closer together. A valley opened in front of me. Long, dried-up grass stalks in yellows and browns, green leaves; beyond that, grey and purple peaks.

Build my church here.

Stones appeared from nowhere. Great blocks of rock, the colour of the mountains. A tidy stack of slates, the colour of the sky. I heard the whine of a cement mixer, saw figures run to and fro. Scaffolding appeared. The sun was hot on my arms and back.

I was sitting on the mountain outside the Saint's cave. On the far horizon, a ragged bank of peaks stood grey and purple against the sky.

Now I knew where. I still did not know why.

Because it is the will of God, I told myself. That should have been enough for anybody. It should have been more than enough for me.

Who was I to question the will of God?

Who was Jacob to question the will of God? I was Jacob. I was in the desert at night, alone. It was cold. The wind whistled and sighed. A shadow rose up next to me, and I clasped it and fought it and finally overcame it. I forced the struggling form down onto the sand, and in the orange light of the rising sun examined its face.

It was my own face that looked back at me. I was looking up at my own face.

'I'll be leaving the day after tomorrow,' she said as we were walking away from the chapel that evening after service.

Sunlight lay on the water like a wide, shining road that appeared to connect us with the mainland.

We reached the fork in the road. She stopped and turned towards me.

'What will you do?'

It was quiet, so quiet. The evening breeze whistled all around us. The waves sighed. From far away, I heard the call of a seagull.

I thought of the voice that I had heard.

I thought of the visions I had been given to see.

I thought of green and golden stalks of grass, purple mountain peaks.

A great noise filled my ears. It was the sound of my blood rushing through me, of my heart beating.

 # Melangell

Died c 590

Melangell was an Irish princess who fled to Wales to escape an unwanted marriage. She lived in the wilderness for fifteen years, until her solitude was disturbed by a prince hunting. The hunted hares sprang to her for protection, and Melangell caused a miracle to happen: all the hunters found themselves rooted to the spot, the huntsman's horn frozen to his lips.

After she released the hunters, the prince granted her freedom from any molestation in the spot she had lived in for so long. Hares are known locally as 'Melangell's lambs'.

Dwynwen

Fifth or sixth century

One of the fifty sons and daughters of King Brychan. A certain Maelon wished to marry her but she rejected him. She dreamt that she was given a drink which delivered her from him, and which turned Maelon to ice. She prayed that he be unfrozen; that all lovers should find happiness in each other (or else be cured of love); and that she herself should never marry. She is – somewhat surprisingly – the patron saint of lovers in Wales. She founded a nunnery on Llanddwyn Island off Anglesey, and was invoked for the curing of animals.

O

I grew up in a big house, a large family. Brothers and sisters
everywhere you turned, and lots and lots of servants, and I
thought I'd never ever get away from there.

I was a loner.

No. I tried to be a loner. When my sisters and my friends
played Weddings and Happy Families and Smacking the
Naughty Baby, with their dolls, I sat in the grounds under a
bush and played Being Alone. For it really to count, I had to
turn slowly all around in a circle and not see anybody. Usually
I cheated by keeping my eyes shut.

My father liked to call himself the King of the District. He
was an Important Man, and he liked his daughters to make
themselves useful by cementing business and political
alliances; oiling the wheels of fortune and finance.

So I knew that at some point in the future, my time would
come, no getting away from it.

I wanted to get away from it.

I very much did not want to be married.

Nobody understood that.

You'll get used to it, my mother said. Everybody gets
married sooner or later.

These are different times, I argued back, the Great War
over and the old Queen long dead and the Pankhursts
triumphant. She did not know what I meant. She'd never
even heard of Women's Suffrage.

Some of my older, married sisters narrowed their eyes
and said they didn't see why I should be spared when
nobody else was.

My father – in a good mood – laughed and said
nonsense, of course you will, I bet you'll get used to it – with
a nasty twinkle in his eye. He did not have much imagination,
and he was not a nice man. But he was amused, and slapped
me fondly, twice.

Some of my younger sisters laughed at me; they were
looking forward to the big day, the beautiful new clothes and
the reception and the honeymoon; all the attention they
would receive.

I thought of the days and the nights afterwards, the rest of
my life.

∞

I had heard of her, of course. The story had travelled, even
across the water, even into rural Ireland. Especially into
rural Ireland.
Women would tell of her and her unwanted bridegroom,
encased in an impenetrable block of ice. And though the
people tried and tried (so the story was told) with hammers
and chisels and blow torches – they couldn't get him out.
A miracle.
It takes a miracle where I come from to get you out of an
engagement, believe me.

Not everybody believed in the miracle.
Or even in her.
They thought it was just a story, make-believe; a sop; not
something that had really happened.
Some said that even if it had, she'd be dead by now, she'd
died years ago.

I grew up in her shadow. In her light.
I wanted to meet her. I believed I would, one day. I could
never picture her dead. How could she be dead when I was
here, waiting for her?

I'll never forget the day my father brought the suitor home.
That's what he called him: *I have a suitor for you.*
He rang from his office, spoke to my mother and told her
to prepare an extra special dinner, then told me to get my
best frock out and wear it that night.
In the evening, he brought the man home, a business
associate, much older than me, not much younger than my
father. I don't think I said a single thing to him all evening
except How Do You Do and More Sauce? And Good Night.
I don't think he noticed. He and my father talked
throughout the meal – of business, of golf, of hunting and
politics. He held muteness to be a virtue in a woman. He told
my father that he thought I'd make him a good wife.

It should have brought me nearer to her, having an unwanted
fiancé of my own. But it didn't.
I could feel her sliding away from me; feel my dream – of
getting away, of going to meet her one day – slide out of my
grasp and flow away, out of reach, almost out of sight.
Almost.
This is the end of me I thought when my father rang
again, some weeks later, to relay the man's proposal.
His words, not mine.
He has asked me to relay his proposal to you.
You wouldn't think it happens these days, but it does; oh,
it does.
I found my tongue shrivelling in my mouth. I found I was
incapable of pronouncing the word No.
I said nothing, which my father interpreted as consent.
This is the end I thought. He will marry me and I will

cease to be me and become his wife. I will cease to be me and
become a Good Christian Woman.
I did not believe in her miracle any more.

My rage and my determination grew stronger and stronger.
The stronger they grew, the smaller they became.
I could feel the strength grow until it was nothing but a
tiny dot inside me, as white and as hot as iron in the village
blacksmith's fire.
I felt a thunderbolt grow inside me the way I could see
children grow inside women's bellies; although I was not
supposed to know how they got there.
The stronger it grew, the smaller it became. I grew white
and silent while the thunderbolt increased its strength. I
thought I would have to burst with it when its time came,
burst and fly asunder like a ball of fire, showering destruction.

I met Maelon Williams one evening at a dance where mothers
took their daughters to be sold into marriage.
He was charming enough as men go, left my toes almost
intact and occasionally even made me laugh with his stories.
He said he liked me. Maybe he did.
But when he asked could he court me, I said No.
It was not a word he was familiar with.
And it didn't stop him, of course. He kept trying, with his
dancing and his pleasant words, his chest puffed out like a
cockerel's. And when even he could see that that was no
good, he led me into the rose garden one night and pinned
me against the romantically crumbling old wall.
I asked you a question once, he said, and you gave me the
wrong answer. This is your chance to get it right. Will you
marry me?

I didn't know what to do.
First I tried to laugh.
Then I tried to reason.
Then I tried not to be very frightened.

The thunderbolt inside me went white cold with rage.
I freed myself from his grasp and froze him with a glance.
I mean literally.
From one minute to the next, Maelon Williams was
encased in a block of ice.
I was free.

∞

I did not believe in her miracle any more, but there had to be
another way. In the end I chose the simplest. I ran away.
I did what hundreds and thousands of Irish girls must
have done. I crossed the sea and went to Britain.
I found a small 'green' community in the Welsh hills, far
away from civilisation. I stayed there for months – which turned
into years. They grew their own produce; they had goats for
milk and cheese, and sheep for wool. The resident herbalist ran
a weekly class – women only – in natural remedies.
I had never heard of women's shelters, or of women's rights.
I had never even heard of the Ladies of Llangollen.
I began to look after the goats and the sheep and the dogs
and cats; then other people started bringing me their animals.
Soon I had a small herbal animal hospital on my hands.
But I didn't find my true vocation until that night when I
went to my first hunt saboteurs' meeting.
In each hunter I saw my suitor, and I screamed No! at
more of them than I could count. It was a word I had to learn
like a foreign language, like a musical instrument, and I
enjoyed using it in all its nuances. I whispered it and shouted

it, sang it and screeched it; I said it cajolingly and threaten-
ingly, with irony and amusement and joy and in hot fury.
I loved every minute of it.
I was free.

Ꝋ

But I had no idea what to do next.

I tried to imagine explaining to my mother (to Maelon's
mother, for that matter) what had happened. I wasn't sure
which bit they would find harder to believe: the fact that the
most eligible bachelor of Cwmcapel had tried to force me, or
the fact that I had deep-frozen him for his pains.

Of course he'd never do that, my dear. You must have
imagined it. Are you sure you haven't had a drop too much
of that French wine?

Come on now, dear, unfreeze him. You've had your joke,
and I'm sure I don't know how you did it. Very clever, of
course. But think how cold the poor boy must be by now.

God, but he looked stupid, even through inches of ice.

In the end, I left him there in the rose garden and just
walked away.

It was a lovely summer's night, warm and balmy and
smelling of hay and dust and, faintly, salt and seaweed.

I walked and walked, and when morning came I had
arrived at the seashore. There was a small island just off the
coast, and I took off my satin shoes that were falling to bits,
hitched up what was left of my dress and waded across.

Finally alone.

There was a well with sweet water on the island, and wild
brambles and even an apple tree.

Finally alone.

Over the years, I don't quite know how, I acquired a

reputation as a wise woman who could make and unmake spells, see into the future and cure afflictions in humans and beasts.

I suppose the story of what had happened to Maelon helped a bit.

It was mostly women who came to see me and ask me for advice. I gave them my apples and a drink from the well, and they left, strengthened and comforted, and spread the word.

For twenty years and more, I was happier that I'd ever been. After that, I sometimes dreamed of the world again. Never of Cwmcapel, and not often of other places, but just sometimes I wondered what it might be like somewhere else, across the water in other countries. What it might be like meeting other people.

I had companions, of course. There were the seals who'd lie for hours on the rocks in the sun, and at night threw off their skins and came ashore to dance.

There were birds, crows and gulls mostly, who would sit in the tree and entertain me with stories of what they'd seen and heard.

There were quite a few cats, and a couple of donkeys and an old, wise, moth-eaten sheep.

After another twenty years, I decided I needed a change from my island life. I packed some ripe apples, filled a flask with water and waded ashore for the first time in four decades. I turned round and round with my eyes closed and finally chose a direction that seemed promising.

CD

They didn't like it, of course. And not just the hunters. In some places it was half the village that would slam its doors in our faces when we came to shop for something that we couldn't grow, or to visit a friend or the library. Some men

spat when they saw us; and even some of the children jeered.
If we thought a fox or a hare or a bird was that important,
they said, we could go and ask *them* for ink or butter or clothes.
But they still brought their animals to us when the vet had
given them up.
Then we heard rumours of what they called a counter attack.
They came one morning, quite early; a group of horsemen, and women too, in pink coats, all thundering hooves
and sweaty, nervous horses and baying dogs. They scared the
goats and the sheep and the sick animals in the hospital.
They scared us, too, with their lashing words and the way
some of them looked at us, looked us over. I'd never realised
before in quite that way that we were all of us women in the
community. I didn't think the pink-coated, purple-faced
women would be much help.
My hands were shaking, and I'm not at all sure how much
of that was rage and how much fright.
All I could think was No, no, no.
But I couldn't do a thing.
Then from somewhere sprang a frightened rabbit, white
tail bobbing madly as it tried to run for safety.
Somebody raised a gun, and laughed.
'*No!*' I roared. The bullet stopped in mid-flight.
Nobody moved.
Nothing moved.
Nothing at all.
I scooped up the rabbit and held it for a moment, feeling
its rapid heartbeat.
When I set it down, I caught a movement at the edge of
the trees. It was somebody walking. Coming towards us.
A woman, older than me, quite a bit older, plump and
sunburnt; walking with long, easy strides.
She took in the scene in front of her, stopped at one of the
hunters and snapped her fingers in his face. He made no move.
She laughed.

I couldn't take my eyes off her.
I swear the trees rustled and whispered although the wind
never stirred, and everything around me sang, blackbirds and
skylarks and nightingales and wrens and banshees, and the
vixens in the hills shrieked and howled with joy.
I knew who she was.
I had spent half my life waiting for her. I had never
entirely stopped dreaming about her.

I couldn't take my eyes off her. She was a blazing fire. Sparks
flew from her hair and her finger tips. Her eyes shone
brighter than the sunlight.
I leapt into the flames.

We left the hunters where they were. The horses and dogs
had woken up soon enough and wandered away, bemused
but unharmed. The hunters had been turned to stone.
Learned people are even now travelling to the remote spot
and writing about the discovery of a hitherto unknown stone
circle in the hills of North Wales. Some of the more enlight-
ened ones ask the women in what they call the New Age
community nearby whether the stones hold any religious
significance for them, and the women speak of a miracle.
Then they laugh at the scientists who try to explain to
them about rope pulleys and slides and wooden rollers.

She's teasing me for my old-fashioned language. But darling,
I say. What do you expect? I have been living alone for so
long. I was born back in the Dark Ages. I am an old woman.
Not that old, she replies, laughing, and kisses me. Not that
old.

rganhell

Sixth century

Arganhell, or Arianell, was the daughter of a man of royal family in the early sixth century, in Gwent. She was said to have been possessed by an evil spirit and was kept in bonds by her family for fear she would throw herself into the river or into the fire; and to keep her from biting and tearing her clothes and the people about her. Her illness was cured by St Dyfrig (St Dubricius) who cast out the evil spirit. After her miraculous recovery Arganhell devoted herself to God for the rest of her life.

There is a stream in Monmouthshire that was once called Arganhell.

you are Arganhell.

I know that because you answer when I call you, although I cannot understand what you are saying. You talk to me. They take the body out here every day and tie it down so that it does not move, and then they go away and I don't see them again until evening.

You are Arganhell. You talk to me and sometimes you throw glinting lights into the body's eyes that dazzle them so that they can't see. Your waters mumble and sigh and rush over the stones, they tinkle and they laugh; but their laughter does not hurt. People's laughter hurts and I want to hurt them back. I want to cut their throats to stop the laughter getting into their mouths; once I almost cut the laughter out of a man's belly because that's where it starts; there is a place in the belly where laughter is made and then it rises up inside the body, through the throat and out of the mouth and you can hear it and see it and it causes pain. I wanted to cut his belly open so I could see where the laughter started, to stop him laughing at me ever again but they stopped me instead; they crushed the hand that held the knife and twisted the arms and bound them and they dragged the body out to sit beside you, Arganhell, day after day. Your waters giggle and laugh but the laughter does not hurt.

Sometimes I think you listen and then fear rises like a great noise; when I think you are listening and you know all my thoughts in your cold clear water. Then my thoughts fly away and I look at the stones under the water, grey and black and silver, others a dull red like the dried blood on my clothes once a month. When the bleeding started I didn't know what it was; long ago when I was still living in the body, I remember I used to say *my body* as if it was mine, I must have thought it was mine then. That was before I died. I didn't know how to die properly, that's why nobody has noticed yet. Or perhaps they have and they only pretend.

They have noticed something, they're afraid of the body now; they tie it up so that it can't move.

Isn't that funny Arganhell, they're afraid of the body that's afraid of them.

When the bleeding in the body that I then thought was mine started, I didn't know what it was; I remember I thought I was dying and I was afraid; there must have been a time when I was afraid of being dead, Arganhell, isn't that strange. I went on bleeding, one day two days three days and still the blood, and then I told my mother and her mouth twisted and she said it's because you're old enough, that's what it's going to be like from now on.

And when her brother, my uncle, started coming into my corner of the hall at night she said the same thing. You're old enough now. And her mouth twisted and she looked as though she was remembering something and she looked pleased.

That's when I knew it was just a body, Arganhell, not mine, not me, just a body.

Your water is mumbling to itself and the stones make clinking sounds like music. There is a piece of slate with sharp edges lying near one of the hands.

I watch the fingers twist and strain against the ropes and the hand free itself, I watch as the arm slips out of the rope and the hand grips the piece of slate with the sharp edges and puts the pointed end against the white inner skin of the other arm and presses down hard, and I watch as it slides the sharp edge against the skin and there is a thin red line where the slate has passed. Red, not grey like the slate. You'd think a grey stone would leave a grey line not red, wouldn't you Arganhell, but the line is red; and as the slate slides along the skin again and again there are red droplets forming and then there is a thin line of pain like a wail, and for a short while the body can feel something; even I feel something for a moment as I sit perched inside the head looking out through the eyes that are sometimes dazzled by the glinting of your waters, Arganhell. That's how I know I'm not quite dead yet, because sometimes I can still feel something and the dead feel nothing. Not even when you cut their bodies; I tried that once when I first knew that I was dead but nobody took any notice. I knew that when somebody is dead people will take notice, and lay the body out and wash it and paint it and burn it and put the ashes in an urn and bury that. Nobody had done anything like that with my body although I knew I was dead; I knew I was dead even though I could still feel something when I pushed the point of a knife into my skin and saw red blood come out. But I was old enough for bleeding so I thought, perhaps I will still bleed even though I am dead now. I wasn't sure so I tried it out when one of the slave women had died, I pushed a knife through her skin and into her flesh but she didn't bleed and her face didn't move and her eyes stayed open and wouldn't look at me. She was dead and I wanted to be like her, but she wouldn't tell me how; I sat beside her all night and talked to her and asked her and asked her and then I became angry with her and shouted at her, and I pushed the knife into her because she couldn't feel anything and I wanted to be like that and she wouldn't tell me how.

In the morning my mother's brother who is my uncle found me and he laughed at what I had done and said, you have come too late, I killed her first. And he kicked the dead body and he laughed again and took me away with him. And all the time while he lay on top of the body that I knew then wasn't mine I thought, I have become like him, he killed a woman with cruelty and then I killed her again; he has killed me and he feels nothing of what he does and soon I will feel nothing at all but I will still not be dead.

The piece of slate has fallen to the ground, and I watch the hand snake towards it and pick it up again, and I watch as the pointed end is pressed into the skin of the arm, of the thigh, I watch as the hand scrapes the ragged edge over the shinbone and the back of the other hand; but this time I feel nothing at all, and I hear nothing at all as they come to fetch me in for the night when it's dark. I see their mouths opening and closing and see them point at the piece of slate and while one of them tightens the ropes so the fingers won't be able to find their way out again, another bends down and picks up the slate and flings it into the water, your water Arganhell; will you look after it for me because I will need it again tomorrow.

ᐃᐃᐃ

This day is cold, there is no light glinting on the water but there is water in the air, falling in droplets out of the sky; they have no colour, like blood does, they are cold not warm and they taste of nothing. There are large grey shapes in the clouds moving slowly like ghosts and the trees on the hill shiver because they are cold.

I can hear something moving in you Arganhell, thumping and splashing and metal clinking against your stones and many footsteps.

All day long the body sits and waits and the fingers pinch the legs that are white and blue with the cold in the air, and watch how long it takes the tired blood to flow back into the white pinch marks. When you pinch a dead body there are no pinch marks because the dead don't feel anything.

One day I will be dead and the body will be dead and everything will be over.

ᐃᐃᐃ

I can hear the clinking again Arganhell, and the splashing and the thumping in your waters. There is a long line of horses and they dip their hooves into you one after the other and walk through your waters and clink against your stones and walk out on the other side, the side where the body is sitting and where I am watching them through its eyes.

But they never arrive here, as soon as they touch dry land they dissolve like the ghosts in the clouds, and there is nothing left here, not even a mist.

I watch the stones in the water, grey and black and silver like smoke, others a dull red like dried blood. There is the sound of crying in my head, and I watch the body start to sway, and beat itself and its head against a tree; the bark is rough and damp and smells dark green, and there is a thump, thump, thump that drowns out the crying and after a while there is nothing at all except the thump, thump and the swaying and there is a patch of pain that spreads through the head and the arm and the shoulder of the body, nothing much but I can almost feel it and after a while I forget the crying and I'm dead again.

ΔΔΔ

I cannot hear the clinking this time, or the splashing in your water, Arganhell, but I can see the line of horses and men coming just like before. They stop at the other bank and look for the ford and then one of the men shrugs his shoulders and his mouth opens so I know he is saying something although I can't hear his voice. Then the first horse puts its feet in your water, Arganhell. It snorts and it is afraid of the rushing waters because it was nearly drowned once in a cold mountain stream. It paws the water and makes the stones clink and goes backwards, and I wonder do the hooves hurt you, Arganhell, do you feel it when something walks through you, because you are alive.

I leave the body and then I am on the other bank with the horse, and I can see the body still sitting under the tree, eyes staring like dead but they're not dead yet, not yet. Do not be afraid of Arganhell, I say to the horse. I can see the fear in its belly and I breathe into its nostrils, Do not be afraid of

Arganhell, and then the horse puts its feet into the water and walks forward, and I am sitting under the tree again with the body, watching the line of horses and men cross your waters, Arganhell.

There is a man in the long line of horsemen. He looks different from the others. All the other men take one quick look at the body and then they look away again; there is fear in their eyes and in their bodies, they look away and then they walk away and pretend they have not seen. They will forget that they have seen the body, and then it will be as if it had never been, as if I had never been. That is almost as good as being dead.

But the man who is not like the others has seen the body, and he looks at it and he looks at me and he knows that I am inside it. He looks straight through its eyes and looks at me. He knows that I am there.

He says, do not be afraid, just like I said to the horse. Do not be afraid. And he stoops and takes out a knife and I think he is going to help me and kill me and then I will be dead. He sees the look in the body's eyes and puts the knife away, and squats down and undoes the ropes with his fingers. There are a lot of knots and they are tied fast, it takes him a long time and all the while I can hear his breathing and smell his sweat and I am afraid, afraid.

It takes him a long time as he undoes one knot after the other, while the line of horses and men goes past. One of the horses stops and the man sitting on its back opens and closes his mouth and talks to the man who is untying the ropes, and the man answers him and shakes his head, and then the man on the horse's back shakes his head too and kicks the horse's sides and the horse walks on.

The ropes slide away like snakes, down the body and off the body's arms and legs and I can see the hands opening and closing but nothing else moves.

The man gets up from his crouch and opens his mouth and speaks but I don't hear him. He goes to the edge of the water,

and he scoops up some of your water, Arganhell, in his hands
and brings it to where the body is sitting, and holds the hands
to the body's lips. They are cracked and dry, the mouth is dry
with thirst; and then they part and dip in the water, your water,
Arganhell, and drink, and cold silver runs into the mouth and
down the throat and into the stomach. He helps the body get
up and stagger to the water's edge, and he says... *name?*

I point one of the body's hands at the water and say your
name, Arganhell, because that is the only name I know. He
nods and gets into the water, and takes some in his hands again
and pours it over my head; there is cold silver water running
down the long tangled hair of the head, dripping down from
the neck onto the back and the chest of the body, down, down
all the length of the body.

Arganhell, he says. And *In the name of the Holy Ghost.*

He pours more water onto my head and combs the matted
hair out with his fingers very gently, as though the body wasn't
almost dead, as though it mattered whether or not there was
pain. He combs out all the tangles and the knots in the same
way he undid all the knots in the ropes, and he makes a fire and
burns the ropes.

And then he walks away and I am still sitting under the tree
beside your waters, Arganhell, but now some of your water is
inside the body and some of it is on the outside of the body,
dripping down from the long wet hair on its head; and the taste
of your water is still on the tongue in its mouth. The ropes are
gone from the body, it can move now and it dips its hands into
your waters, Arganhell, to find the slate with the sharp edges.

But as they dip into the water there is a tingling in them,
and they move and there is a feeling of silver and of swiftness
as the water moves between the fingers, and the current tugs at
them, this way and that. As they pull out of the water there is a
flash as drops of water fall from the fingers back into the
stream, and a coldness as the air touches the wet hands; and
then they're in the stream again, feeling cool and silvery and

playing with the currents. The sun comes out of the clouds and there is warmth on the face and on the body and, as I take the hands out of the water and hold them up into the light, there is warmth on them too, all mixed together with the wetness and the drops falling from them back into the stream; back into your waters Arganhell, that gleam and glint like sunlight.

I open the mouth and I say your name again, *Arganhell*, and cup the hands and scoop up water and lift it to the mouth and I drink; I am so thirsty, Arganhell. And I cup them again and bring up more water and lift up the hands and pour the water over my head so that it drips down from the hair all over the body and I can feel it, drip-dripping down, wet like silver, wet like water.

I sit and listen and there is a thumping somewhere inside the body; I stop breathing so that I can hear it more clearly and the thumping gets louder and louder; it comes up the body into the throat, and then it is roaring in my ears and I let out the breath in a long *whoosh* and put a hand on the throat where the thumping was loudest, and there it still is, throbbing through the skin of the neck. I sit there for a long time with a hand on the throat feeling and listening to the thump and throb.

Then I take the hand away and sit just watching it as it opens and closes; I watch the knuckles come up white through the skin as the hand clenches and disappear again as it unclenches; I see red crescent moons where the fingernails have pressed into the skin of the palm. I lift the other hand and put its fingers into the palm, on to the red crescent moons and I stroke them slowly, like I remember the man passing his fingers through my hair. The skin of the palm is warm and soft and moist with sweat. The back of the hand is smoother and cooler; I can feel the bones and the veins through the skin and as I press a finger down on the vein the blood stops flowing and after a while there is a bump and a throbbing, until I take the finger away again and the blood can go on flowing. I follow the line of the vein until it disappears into the crook of the elbow. There is a thin red line on the inside of the arm that is covered by a scab, it makes a rasping sound as I pass a finger over it; and there are thin needles of pain as I pick it off.

The inside of the other arm is very soft and on the outside there are hairs, but very soft and dark, not hard and yellow like the hairs on the arm of my mother's brother who is my uncle. I stroke the hairs, down and down and down like I once remember stroking a cat on the threshold of the great hall in the sunshine.

There is sunshine now, Arganhell, on your waters that glint and gleam like silver; and on the arm of the body that is my arm, Arganhell. The sunshine is warm and I try to purr like the cat purred when I stroked it but there is only a croaking in my throat; perhaps I have forgotten how to purr, perhaps I can only hiss and spit now.

I move the hand up the arm and over the shoulder and on to the neck, and the other hand too; they encircle the neck and there is a pain around the throat where the croaking is; a pain all around the inside of my throat that grows tighter and tighter and I can't breathe. My hands stroke the neck and I make the croaking sound again; I remember sitting in the sunshine on the threshold of the great hall with the cat that was purring because it was happy and it liked me; and I remember that I was happy, a long time ago when I was still alive, like you are alive, Arganhell. The pain in my throat gets worse and worse and the croaking gets louder and louder and I can't breathe.

I say your name and I lie down and dip my face into your waters and drink and the cold silver water runs down my throat. There is water now in my face but salty, not sweet like your water, and it is warm not cold. And the croak in my throat turns into a roar and the body is rocking and swaying as if a big hand was holding it and shaking it; and everything hurts, Arganhell.

ᐤᐤᐤ

I think what I am doing is crying; I remember I used to cry a long time ago when I was still alive, and now I sit and cry for a long time by your waters and then I sit and watch the water stream past and then I fall asleep.

When I wake up one hand is numb and I hold it with the other; it begins to crawl like ants and I am afraid and I shake it and shake it to shake off the ants, and the crawling stops. One side of my face is hot from the sun and the other is cold from the soil and the grass that it has lain on. I lift a hand and pass it over the face; there are the shapes of blades of grass on the skin of this side of the face; the skin is cool and damp and there is a green smell on my fingers. The skin round the eyes is hot and dry and the lashes are like fine grass. The hair of the eyebrows is smooth and dry under my fingertips. I listen to your waters talking and mumbling and laughing and telling me stories while I sit for a long time stroking first one eyebrow and then the other, stroke, stroke, stroke.

The skin of the forehead is cold and my hand feels warm on it. The hair is still wet; I smooth my hands down it like the man did, slowly, gently, down and down and down until it is all dry. I take a strand of it in my mouth and it tastes salty and bitter and warm.

And then my feet twitch and I get up and I walk a few steps, slowly because it is so long since the body walked by itself, without being dragged or pushed. I walk a few steps away from the water and then I walk the same steps back and alongside you because I don't like not being near you, Arganhell. I have been with you for so long.

The feet are uncertain, they are clumsy and they stumble but they walk on, not as fast as your waters are flowing but they walk on.

After a long time they stop by the water's edge and my legs fold and I am crouching over you and looking into your water and there is a face looking up at me. Its lips are moving, my lips are moving, and I say,

I am Arganhell.

Eiliwedd

Sixth century

Also known as Almedha, Aled or Eluned.
One of the many sons and daughters of
King Brychan of South Wales.

She was expected to marry a certain
prince of a neighbouring kingdom, but
would not do so and ran away from home
instead. She attempted to hide herself in
rags in three villages, but was hounded
out of each as a thief or a vagrant. Later,
plagues from heaven were visited upon all
three villages. Eiliwedd finally convinced
the lord of a manor near the town of
Brecon to let her stay as a hermit in a
simple hut on his estate and give her alms
to live on. But the prince (or, in other
versions of the legend, her father) finally
found Eiliwedd, and when she refused to
come back with him he beheaded her. A
spring is said to have welled up at the spot
where she was murdered.

1 knew her.

I used to know her. When she was still alive.

The sound of her footsteps follows me wherever I go.

They feed me well, the people in the *llys*, god knows why. She sometimes said that. *God knows why*. Perhaps her god does know.

She said as far as she knew, he knew everything. Omniscient, she said, was the word for that. He was, so she'd been taught, everywhere at once. Omnipresent, she said. That's what you call that.

Always tried to teach me words, that girl. Always tried to learn words off me too. What do you call this bird, what's the word for that bush, that animal here, that thing there? Didn't teach her much behind those castle walls, did they?

Not the right things, anyway, if you ask me.

Not that you would.

Who'd ever ask me anything, other than how much for a quick hour in the hay or the grass, or the pig-sty? They know it won't be much I'll ask.

But that's all over.

I used to know her, when she was still alive. I used to think I liked her, in the sort of way you like a cat or a dog you can't eat. Not much use, but a bit of company maybe.

I used to think she liked me too. I could be useful to her you see, showing her the things her booklearning hadn't even mentioned.

I did lose patience with her more than once; she was so nice and so slow, that girl; didn't understand anything. Didn't understand that you have to kick them before they can think of kicking you; didn't understand that begging is good but stealing is better; because their contempt hurts less when you've done something contemptible – other than just existing and getting in people's way, I mean.

She never understood that.

I used to think it was because life must have been so different for her; maybe her people were so rich that even girl children were welcome there and treated well.

I found out after a while that it had not been so. They'd treated her like everybody else treats their daughters. But then, she'd rarely gone hungry; not really; not like rats biting and tearing at your insides and the fear that this time it's going to be the last and you're going to die; and then worse than the fear, the not caring. That's the last thing before the pains start, and after the pains are done with you, you die.

She didn't know about things like that.

She knew about words, and stories from that book all about her god who she said was everywhere and knew everything.

I can hear her footsteps again. She is walking on the wind.

She was so young.

Two years younger than me, but she'd never catch up.

Didn't know anything, didn't understand. Not much use except for the company, like a cat or a dog you can't eat, or a tame bird.

Sang like a bird, when she was happy. She sang to her god, but she wouldn't sing to earn us some bread.

I understood that; I hate people gawking and measuring you up with their eyes, the men for a quick lay and the women because they see their men look at you like that. What you think doesn't count; what you are nobody's interested in.

Who you are, she said one evening when I went on like this. Not what.

You may be a *who*, I told her, but I'm a *what*, that I know for a fact, and so are you now you're on the road like the rest of us.

She smiled at me and shook her head, and stretched out her arm and gave me something she'd been working on with her clever white fingers; a necklace she'd made from acorns and horse chestnuts and bird feathers and shells from the river.

For you, she said. It will look beautiful against your skin.

Maybe she'd just made it and tired of it and wanted rid of it; or perhaps it was to show me that she thought I was a *who*, not a *what*; or maybe she made it for me as a gift because she was sweet and a little simple in her head. But all I thought of was the bread she could have stolen instead; the hares she could have snared or the fish caught; or even the men she could have earned a few coins from, although that was something even I only did when there was nothing else, and she, never.

But there she sat, smiling as if she was pleased with herself, with me; as if I should be pleased with her; when all I could think of was being always hungry and cold and never having a place to go home to.

You silly little bitch, I said, then shouted; you simple-minded useless piece of woman-flesh, and I tore the necklace out of her hand and broke the string and scattered acorns and horse-chestnuts and shells everywhere, and feathers flew. Because the truth was that she had reminded me that I was nothing, not even *what*, and I wanted her to stop.

It will look beautiful against your skin she had said, as if *beautiful* and I could go together. Those words of hers were clawing open the graves of things I'd buried long ago and was finally rid of. She was bringing back all the dreaming and the hoping I'd killed off and put away because the pain was too much. So I had to stop her.

She was sweet and simple-minded and didn't understand; and at first I thought I could knock the nonsense out of her like it had been knocked out of me, but I couldn't.

And maybe it hadn't been knocked properly out of me either; because I'd never been much good, and look at me now; a beggar woman after all. And I think I've done well for myself.

The shadows gather; twigs are cracking under the tree.
Who's there?
But it's only me and her ghost.
Only me.

I didn't see her for a while after that time with the necklace.
        She ran away from me and I don't blame her; she was a runner-away, that's why she was still around. She was sweet, and simple in her head, but she did know some things about looking after herself. She knew better than to stay with a woman who'd lay into her like I did that night.
        She never fought back, or even screamed. She just curled up until it was all over, her hands holding her head; and then she looked at me and got up and backed away; and then she turned round and ran away into the dark.
        She had more sense than to stay with someone who'd beat her like I had done that night.
        She had more sense than me. I had stayed with someone like that until I'd been kicked out; and even then I'd hung around the door hoping to be let back in. No pride.
        She told me that in the castle, they'd taught her that pride was wrong.
        They'd taught her that her god had said that if someone hit her on the one cheek, she had to turn her other one as well; not run away or fight.
        Stupid, I told her. Fight, that's what you have to do. Running is for cowards.

I've not been able to do either.

I can't turn the other cheek, she said, in a serious voice, as if she was really thinking about it. I would like to, but I couldn't. Maybe if I'd had the choice...

They beat you at home, in the castle? I asked. I'd never met a girl that's not been beaten, as a child or later, when she would bring shame over the family. Boys people are sometimes careful with, if it's an only son; but if a girl dies from a beating, there's money saved and one husband less to find.

Yes, she whispered, as if it was something shameful.

I could see that she'd kept her dreams and her hoping; she'd not killed them and buried them like I had. She'd kept the pain too, and it was hurting her then.

What was that? But there's nothing there. It's only the little stream whispering to itself. Not far to the *llys* now, to the big wooden doors where I'll stand with my face covered and in the shadows, begging for a crust of bread. They feed me well, but I have to come here every day and ask them, hold up the cage and show them my pride is still safely locked up inside it; no chance of it getting out and incommoding them.

Incommode. That's another of her words; she used it once, when I'd only known her a few weeks; and then she laughed and said she'd never have to say that word again, because now she was free.

The wind is rustling in the trees and the dry grass, snapping and sighing in the branches like voices arguing.

Sometimes I wish she'd come back and haunt me, properly I mean, so that I could see and touch her; and hear more than just her footsteps following me.

There's only her invisible ghost here now; only her ghost and the wind stalking through the dry grass.

I didn't see her for a while after she'd run away from me; I thought I'd never see her again, but a few weeks later she turned up again. The group I was with had gone on to another little market town, and there she was, on the market, driving geese and suckling-pigs for the farmers, helping herself to apples and loaves of bread and smiling at everyone.

I remember thinking, there she is, stealing like me now, bold as brass. She's learned something; maybe I've beaten some wisdom into her. Then she turned round and vanished in the crowds, and I thought maybe I'd imagined her there after all, because I wanted to see her.

But I met her again a few days later; and she hadn't been stealing at all that day I saw her. She'd found work in the *llys* of a local prince and the other servants had taken her to the village on market day.

But you're from the big castle in the town, I said, and now you work in a place not half the size of your castle?

Yes, she said, and laughed with her teeth showing. And, see, they even give me money for it! At home, I had to do work and all I got was my sisters boxing my ears and my Lord Father coming into my bed at night...

She stopped, I could see that she hadn't meant to say that. Then she talked on, about how her new lord believed in her god too, and let her go on believing and do her singing and her praying in peace. And she said again that she was happy, and she was free.

If I don't like it here, she said, I'll move on, live on the road again, like you, find other work. Are you not happy for me?

I did not tell her what I thought, that I do not think you can be in somebody's pay and still be free. She was sweet, and a little simple in her head, but even she would have seen that I was crying down what I could never have. And also I could not forget her face when she held up the necklace for me; and the way it changed when I started cursing her, and beating her.

So I tried to smile for her and marvelled that she should not be afraid of me. But perhaps now that she had a place in the world again and even owned something she'd honourably come by, she felt that I was less of a threat to her. I who was nothing.

Early the next morning I woke up from the place I had found for myself to sleep, in a stable. There was a commotion in the street, screaming and yelling. I stumbled outside. It was cold, the sky green and pale blue.

A knot of people was standing in the middle of the street. There were shouts of 'Thief' and 'Robber'; and some people were throwing stones. I heard another voice, screaming and crying, 'No, no...' and then the *thwack* of another stone hitting its mark.

I'd been caught like that once, and I'd been lucky to run away. This one wasn't so lucky.

I craned my neck and sidled my way through the crowd; and there she was lying on the ground, holding on to a chicken, hiding her head in her hands but it was no good; I'd only been using my hands on her, but these were heavy stones with sharp edges, and already there was blood running through her fingers, and although her legs were still twitching and her body writhing she'd stopped crying. Stopped making any sound.

I stood there, knowing I should help her, and also knowing in my bones that I was too late, or that soon now would be too late; that nobody would listen to me; I who was known to be a thief and a vagrant; who'd believe me if I told them that she was sweet and simple and happy not to have to steal any more? And still I wish, oh how I wish I had spoken; she might have heard me turning my cheek to protect her, she might have known that there was someone on her side, someone who knew her. She would have known that I was sorry I had beaten her. You shouldn't hurt something that wants to be free if you have no need, she'd once said when she let the rabbit in our snare escape. I'd beaten her for that too, but not very much because I knew that she wanted to be free and she thought that I did too. She didn't know that it was too late for me.

So I stood there doing nothing until it was too late for her and she was dead.

I was still standing there when all the people had left, the excitement being over.

I couldn't bear her being dead.

She was the only one who'd ever looked at me as if I was somebody.

She couldn't be dead.

I went back the way she had come, stealing a chicken on the way. I didn't know if she'd been taking the one she'd held in her hand to her new lord's cook, or whether she'd decided to run away and had taken it with her.

I stole a chicken and took it back to her lord's cook; I didn't want them to think she was a thief. I was going to tell them that she wasn't.

But the man didn't even look at me; he snatched at the bird and cursed because I was late and boxed my ears.

He thought I was her; he didn't know what she looked like. He'd not even looked at her and he didn't look at me.

So I stayed, because for as long as I took her place and did her work, people wouldn't know that she was dead. She wouldn't really be dead, because I was the only one who knew.

So I stayed; but then after a while I couldn't bear it when people saw me or looked at me. I heard more about her god and the stories people told about him; and I thought there must be a sign on my forehead like on the forehead of Cain who killed his brother Abel in one of the stories; because I had stood and watched and let them kill her. I had beaten her although I know that she would not hurt anyone.

People's looks began to hurt me like blows. I would cower down and cover my head in my hands the way she had.

Finally I went to the holy man in the *clas* and told him I had heard told stories of other women and men who'd wanted to devote themselves to the god and gone to live somewhere in the wilderness all by themselves; and how I wished I could go and live in the wilderness all by myself too.

He looked at me long, and then he went and talked to the lord of the *llys* and came back to me and said that I could, only I'd have to build my own hut and come to the *llys* gates every midday for my bread, to learn humility.

I am doing what I think she would have wanted, because she always said she wanted to be free, even if I think she sometimes didn't know how to.

I can almost feel her next to me, every day, her ghost haunting me and being company; because I must never forget what I have done.

Maybe that's her feet now I can hear rustling in the grass, snapping twigs.

But it's not her; I can see it's a man on a horse coming towards me, and all of a sudden I am running, stumbling down the hillside while behind me the horse's hooves are thundering on the dry earth and I can hear it coming, closer, closer, closer.

The man is calling her name, my name now, Eiliwedd! Eiliwedd!

There's the ford across the stream; once I'm past that, it's not far to the *llys* gates. But the horse is much, much faster than I am.

I'm in the water, breathing in gasps because I am so afraid; my feet are slipping on the pebbles in the water and the current is tugging at my legs; and behind me I can hear the man's voice.

Eiliwedd! It's no good trying to run away, I always told you. I always told you I'd come after you, and I'd get you in the end, and now I have. This is for you, Eiliwedd you little whore, for going against me.

There's something whistling though the air and then pain explodes on the side of my neck and I stumble in the water and fall; and the horse splashes past me.

I can't breathe, my neck hurts like it did that time
someone was trying to strangle me, tighter and tighter.
There's a pounding in my ears and a voice that whines,
Eiliwedd, Eiliwedd, help me, help me.

My feet are cold from the water, my legs, my whole body;
all I am now is the pain and a voice that whimpers her name.

cold, cold water, cold cold i'm so cold
cold is better than the pain that is everywhere.
   Dead.
   I think I am dead, I wish I could see Eiliwedd again and tell
her that I died for her, and ask her to forgive me.

When I open my eyes again it's dark; I can hear the water in the
stream rushing and I'm cold, so cold; and there's a terrible pain
in the side of my neck whenever I move, whenever I breathe.
   I'm not dead.
   I'm still alive and Eiliwedd is still dead.

ᐃᐃᐃ

I have left my hut on the hill. I can't stay now that she is dead
again, and everyone knows it.
   Her story is being told now, just like all those god stories in
the book that she told me about.
   People tell her story as if she was someone they'd made up.
How she ran away from home so she wouldn't have to marry
the man her father chose for her. How she lived in Christian
poverty but was run out of villages because people thought she
was a thief, homeless, a woman of the road; and how her god
later sent plagues to those villages, to punish them. How she
finally found charity with a big lord who let her live on his land,
and how the man she'd refused to marry - others say it was her
father himself - went after her. And how she defended her
chastity and died for it.

Everybody knows she's dead now; they heard the man brag about how he'd killed the bitch that had gone against his orders. Someone saw me lie in the stream, white and bleeding from the neck. They wouldn't want me to be alive now. Maybe they wouldn't even want her to be alive. When I got up and crawled away, they just said it was a miracle; her dead body disappearing like that.

They're beginning to call her a saint, not because she was sweet and tried to be free and not to harm anybody; but because they say she was a virgin, and because she is dead.

Yesterday I began to collect acorns and horse chestnuts and shells from the stream for a necklace. I hope she can see me. I hope she can forgive me for having twice stolen her life.

I miss her.

Eurgain

eurgain (obsolete) *adj* – of golden brightness, golden and beautiful

Eurgain was the daughter of Prince Caratacus (Caradog) of Glamorgan. Around 50 AD, he and his family were taken to Rome as captives in the wake of the Roman conquest of Britain.

In Rome, Eurgain is believed to have taken on the revolutionary new Christian faith. When she returned to Wales some years later, she brought the religion and, so the story goes, a group of Christians with her and started spreading the word. This would make her the first missionary in Britain.

Many women in the early church were active as deacons, preachers and missionaries: either alone, in pairs or with their husbands.

Her church came to be called Côr Eurgain or Bangor Eurgain. It was already an old place by the time – some 400 years later – that Saint Illtud came to live there. Today, Côr Eurgain is known by his name: Llanilltud Fawr, Llantwit Major.

Arddun! *Arddun!!*

They said you might get here today. It is so good to see you!
How long has it been – six years?

Come on! Let's go down to the beach and talk.

I've only been back a couple of weeks; me and Grandfather, we
travelled together. Mother and Father and Gwyn and Einir and
Gwladus are still in Rome. Gwladus got married last year.

She's fine, doing really well. She changed her name to
Claudia. You know. More Roman.

Oh, come on. Rome's OK.

No, really. It's a great place.

It's HUGE. Look at that field there, and that, and that one,
and then that hill and those two over there as well. And now
imagine they're all covered with stone streets and stone houses,
and crowded with people. That's how big just *one* of the
quarters of Rome is.

There are houses there, higher than trees. In the
tenements, you walk up flights of stairs, up and up and up like
a mountain. Some of those houses have five or even six
storeys! They are called *insulae* - islands, you know - and when
you're on the top floor of one and you've got your breath back
and look out, it is a bit like being on an island; only you're
surrounded by a sea of buildings and people and donkeys and
shouts and smells...

No – I am glad I'm back, honest! And you're still my best
friend in the world, Arddun, of course you are. You don't know
how glad I am to sit here again with you, in the dunes like we
used to when we were kids. It's just... I've been away for six
years – that's nearly half my life. And it's really weird being

back here now. It's like it's almost not home anymore, you know? Everything's so different.

Or, I don't know. Maybe I'm different.

I miss Rome. I know we were there as prisoners really, but that was only in the beginning. Then they let us free, after Father and Mother paid homage to the Empress Agrippina and the Emperor Claudius.

Hades. Don't let Tegau catch me saying that! She doesn't like the thought of any of us paying homage to another king. I don't think she really believes Rome exists....

You remember her, don't you – Tegau, my old nurse? She still thinks I'm a kid, and I'm not! I'm fifteen, a grown woman.

You know I freed Tegau? I freed all my slaves, and I asked Grandfather to free all his. We *pay* them now for what they do, and some of them have left. Imagine! I wouldn't have expected that they would just want to go off like that, after they'd been with us for so long. I mean, I thought they'd be pleased with me about their freedom. Sometimes I almost wish I hadn't freed them. Or that Grandfather had forbidden it. But somehow, I think he understands.

Well, it's because *we* were slaves when we first went to Rome. All of us! We were taken to Rome in chains, because of Mother and Father starting that rebellion against the Romans. You should hear the bard, he doesn't half go on about it. He's written a whole bloody epic. It's all made up though. It's all about how heroic and brave we were, and I can tell you, we *weren't*! First of all there was that really, really awful journey to Rome, on the boat. We didn't know what they would do to us. There were other slaves on board and they said we were going to be a spectacle in the arena – you know, in the circus. Torn apart and eaten by wild animals as the Enemies of Rome, with a huge crowd looking on and roaring and laughing and drinking and farting. And you die and scream with pain...

Sorry.

Didn't mean to be morbid. I just still dream about it, sometimes.

No, no, no, of *course* it didn't really happen, I wouldn't be here otherwise – would I? We were taken to watch once, later, after we were freed, when we were the guests of the empress and emperor.

It was terrible. Oh, Arddun, it was horrible. I think that was when I became a Marian. After, I mean. When we got there, I wasn't even sure what was going to happen at first. I thought it was going to be acrobats, magicians, like those you can see in the streets only much grander. Then the people came into the arena. Criminals, gladiators, men, women... Oh, Arddun, you can't imagine.

But they're not doing it for the gods! It's for *entertainment*, can you believe it? The people in the audience, they were *enjoying* it.

I hated it. I sat there and hated it, and I hated all of them. I kept thinking, this could have been us. Gwladus and Einir and Gwyn and Mother and Father and Grandfather and me, being killed like that. I heard the people in the arena scream and howl for mercy. And then I saw the looks on people's faces around us in the audience. They were really getting off on it.

I threw up on a whole row of them. I wish I could have puked on the whole amphitheatre!

Don't laugh, Arddun, it's not funny. Really it isn't.

No, I'm not crying.

Piss off.

I'm going for a walk.

ᴧᴧᴧ

Oh.

Arddun.

Yeah, I'm fine.

Look. I'm not in much of a mood for talking now. See you tomorrow, OK?

No - it's nothing personal. Honest. It's nothing to do with you.

Learning Resources

Of course I'm still your friend!

Well – it's just... you don't really know me. I mean – you know me from when I was a kid. I was nine when we left here, and I'm fifteen now and... well. I've *changed*, do you know what I mean?

Exactly. We've both changed. And it's really difficult here, you know? I keep forgetting words, I'm probably *thinking* in Latin. It's like I'm half Roman now, and half not.

I missed home so much when we got to Rome. I missed *you*. I didn't have anyone to talk to. I kept thinking about home and missing it and really, really wanted to come back. Only there was no way the Romans would let us go while the fighting here was still going on. We had to wait and wait. And I was really worried as well.

About you! I didn't know if you'd been killed in the fighting or taken captive or *what*!

And now I'm back and it's really weird. It's all so *different*.

I don't know... Like, it's not just that I've changed and stuff, that I'm different from how I used to be. I mean, that too. But I'm *different*, do you know what I mean? I don't fit in. Not in Rome. I'm still a sort of barbarian there. I thought I'd be OK once I got back here again. But now Prydain doesn't really feel like home either.

Oh, Arddun, don't look like that.

I just don't know what I'm going to do now. And Nesmut's bored out of her skull because she can't talk to anyone...

My friend. Nesmut – the one who came with us from Rome.

Yeah, the dark one with the big eyes.

She's not stuck up – she just doesn't understand what people are saying. She only speaks Latin and Greek and Coptic, and that's not going to do her much good here, is it?

What?

Marianism. How do you know about that?

Did I? Oh. Yeah, I think I did. When I was telling you about that godawful circus we went to...

No, I'm not upset.

Yes, OK, I am. It's just... Oh, all right, I'm going to tell you. I knew one of the people there.

One of the people in the arena. One of the gladiators.

Abra.

I couldn't believe it was her there. I'd known she was training to be a gladiator, but the way she'd talked about it, I thought it was all for show. Like dancing, she said it was. Beautiful movements. Skill. A trained body. She said she'd always wanted to be a gladiator.

I sat there and saw her fight and die. And then I was sick and we had to leave.

Oh, Arddun, it was terrible. I sat there and saw her die, and I couldn't do anything.

I still have nightmares about it. I'm there in the arena holding a knife, and she's on the ground with all her wounds and I try to run to her and kill her to stop the pain but I can't move. I can't move. And I wake up and think, Why do I want to *kill* her? She was my friend, she was only a few years older than me. She was my favourite slave in the house and I shouldn't want to kill her in my dream, I should want to save her; but I always want to kill her.

Every time.

After that, I became a Marian. It's a new religion from the East. Mary is a great prophet. She is travelling and preaching all over the Roman empire. She used to travel with another prophet called Jesus, but he was killed. Like Abra.

He hadn't done anything. He was just a good man. A carpenter.

Some of the slaves in Nesmut's house were Marians; they told me about it first. Marianism is about justice and wisdom.

Well, for example, Marians say that *all* people have a spirit. The spirit is the most important part of you. It's the light of Sophia in every one of us that goes back to the sun after we die. Sophia means wisdom. So if everybody has a spirit, it's not fair to keep slaves, right? Because they're the same as you. That's

what Junia says, only she puts it better than that. Junia's a sort
of friend of me and Nesmut – she's an apostle and a preacher
in Rome. An apostle is somebody who follows the path of
Mary and Jesus. I want to be like her, and like Mary.

Mary's not from Rome. She's from a place called Magdala
in the province of Syria. Look, I'll draw a map in the sand for
you. This is Britannia, and Germania and Gallia and Hispania
over there, and Italia here. The sea is called the *Mare Internum*.
Syria's right at the other end of that, there. That's where Mary
comes from. She is from a people called Jews, and most of
those who believe in her and Jesus's religion are Jews too, but
you don't have to be one to be a Marian.

Well – me and Nesmut and Junia for example – we call
ourselves 'Marians', after Mary. And others call themselves
Christians, after Jesus. Because he is also called Christ. Some
believe that he was a god.

No, I don't think so. I think he was the same as Mary – a
prophet. She wants to change things, and so did he. To make
the world better for everybody.

Well, for example, I think if Abra hadn't been a slave she
could have become something other than a gladiator.

Yes, I know, she *did* want to become one, but gladiators are
mostly slaves. There are very few free ones, and even fewer free
women gladiators. So if she'd been free, she could have done
something else. She could have been a bodyguard or a farmer
or a market trader. *Something* else!

She wouldn't have needed to die like that.

So what if she was a slave? She was a *person*! She was my
friend.

I was a slave when we first came to Rome. Me and Gwladus
and Einir and Gwyn and Mother and Father and Grandfather
– we were *all* slaves. We were paraded round Rome in our
chains to show that the emperor'd defeated the barbarians.

Oh, don't be so dense, Arddun. What do you think? *We*
were the barbarians! To the Romans, we're barbarians.

They could have killed us at any moment. Sold us. Raped us. Anything. We were lucky that nothing happened. And then we were really lucky when the emperor and empress set us free after a few years. We didn't *know* they were going to let us go. One moment, Einir and me were being the empress's little pets – she showed us off to guests the same as she did her monkeys and that leopard she kept. And then the next minute it was: you're free! We didn't know what to do. We were so used to obeying commands. That was about three years ago, and I'm sort of beginning to believe that I'm really free now – you know, forever?

It's just so weird, all of it.

I mean, to begin with, I'm a princess in Prydain, right. You know, with my own slaves and clothes and jewellery and stuff. Then suddenly, I'm a captive and I get carted off halfway across the world and become a foreigner and a barbarian. And then I'm a slave. A nobody with nothing. No past, no future. And finally, the most gracious emperor and empress set us free and then I'm a freedwoman, get that, *and* a foreign princess again. And I'm sort of like half a Roman now, but I'm also still a barbarian. Or, you know, people think I am. I mean – that's what makes it so weird. In Rome, they think I'm a barbarian because I'm from Prydain. And here, they think I'm a barbarian because I'm, like, half a Roman, with my clothes and my accent and my hairstyle and stuff.

And I don't know what I am.

I don't even know if I want to stay here or not. I get really homesick for Rome sometimes.

Yes, I know that I said that it can be really horrible there, and there's lots of things wrong with it, and the Romans aren't always that great... but there are people from all over the empire in Rome, loads of different sorts of foreigners; I like that. And all sorts of religions – like Marianism. And for example, we have a *woman* prophet, and priestesses. They're independent. Free. They do what they like. That's unusual.

Well – in Rome, they have different ideas about women.
Very strange ideas. Like, they have an emperor and an
empress, but it's only the *emperor* who has the power.
I don't know. She just sits there and looks pretty. I think
empresses do a lot of secret scheming though, you know? I
heard some stories about an empress who had her husband
poisoned and then had her little son crowned emperor. And
then while the son is small, she is the real ruler; only officially
it's him, even if he's only a baby.

No, I'm not making this up! They were so *rude* to Mother!
Even after they'd set us free, they only ever addressed Father as
Ruler, *never* Mother! She was *so* cross. She nearly beheaded a
couple of guards from the imperial palace. Do you know, they
found *us* peculiar, because we always paid homage to the
emperor *and* the empress.

But now, most of my friends there are Marians, and they're
different. We're all different. Junia, and Nesmut and me. And
Tryphaena and Tryphosa – they're missioners. They go about
and preach the gospel to people who don't know about it yet.
In between their trips, we all meet up. There aren't any Marian
temples in Rome or anywhere else; nothing like that. We meet
in people's houses. Junia has a flat in a tenement, so we often
met there.

Oh, Arddun, I miss those evenings. We'd be all sitting
there in the big room, with the shutters open and the noise
and the food smells from the street coming in. Junia can read,
so she would be reading out letters from other sisters in the
church; or people would come with questions and then we'd
have a discussion.

Oh, you know – about the sayings of Mary and Jesus and
what they meant. For example, Jesus said that the best thing
you can do is to give away all your things and money to the
poor and be free to travel about the country like he did. And
Mary says that having a free spirit and striving for wisdom is
the best thing. So we'd discuss that – can you own things and

be free in spirit? Can you give away everything but still have a spirit that's not free? And what do you do if you have to look after children or your old parents and can't just give it all up and go away? Or when you're a slave? Stuff like that. Philosophical questions. Junia said that talking like that was a way of achieving wisdom. Other times people would come and tell us about their problems, like when someone was ill or they were worried about something, and then we'd all talk about that and try to help. Or sometimes sisters would come from other parts of the empire and tell us what it was like there...

Do you know what I'd *really* like to do, more than anything else in the world? Be a missioner with Nesmut, like Tryphaena and Tryphosa are. I'd love us to travel all through the empire together, see all the different countries and people and learn their languages and tell them about the message of Mary and Jesus. I want to tell people who own slaves why I don't think it's the right thing to do. And I want to tell the slaves that they have a spirit like everybody else. That we should all be free, but that at least in spirit, they can be as free as anybody.

I think that's what life is about. Being as free as you can, and striving for wisdom and justice. For everybody, everywhere.

Indeg

Ninth century

Indeg was the daughter of a Viking chieftain of the Isle of Man. Like her mother before her, she became a Christian in secret. When her father found out, he had his wife killed and made their daughter choose between God and death. Indeg, a martyr to her faith, declared that she would never abjure.

She was put in a boat and set adrift on the sea. The waves carried her miraculously to a spot near Abersoch on the Llyn Peninsula, where she lived as a hermit in a hut on the cliffs. On old maps, the place is still called Llanindeg.

The Christians had come to my mother when she was young. They were wandering monks, two of them, over from Ireland in a tiny boat. They didn't know anything about sailing. 'The Lord guided us to you,' they told her as they landed on the shore at her feet. She was sixteen and impressionable, but it is true that their coracle was washed up on the only bit of sandy beach on miles and miles of rocky coastline. 'The Lord guided us to you.' It would make you feel special, wouldn't it? It did her. She converted on the spot and was baptised in salt water. She would dedicate herself to the new Lord the two strangers had brought. She was already married and pregnant, too late now to give her life to religion in the way they told her was best: pure and virgin. So she decided to do the next best thing and bring up her children in the faith.

There were two sorts of tales my mother told me as I grew up: stories from the Holy Book; and the account of her conversion by the sea and the sayings of the holy Fathers. Of all the children she bore, I was the only one to survive; that made me all the more precious. Mine was the life she was going to give to the Lord; in secret if necessary. My father, who worshipped the old gods, wanted a good marriage for me. He had his eye on a chieftain in the Hebrides, an important man. Family ties with him would be desirable. So I was to make myself useful.

But my mother had other plans. She knew that there was no arguing with my father. She schemed and planned, and finally bribed a fisherman to spirit me away at night to a convent in Ireland. She liked the thought of giving me to Ireland whence had come her own salvation. She never asked me, or herself, whether I would like it. There never was an alternative. I had

known all my life that I was going to be given to the Lord. She
was an obedient wife in everything but this. Perhaps the idea of
martyrdom appealed to her, because of course, once it was
done, there was no hiding the deed from my father.

I didn't learn about her fate until later. For the time being,
there I was on the boat in the middle of the night, the sea calm,
the moon making a bright path on the dark waters, guiding us
to Ireland, to my future in the bosom of the Lord. I knew what
awaited me: a clean, unsullied life in prayer, no distractions
from the world. I was to be luckier than my mother, who had
had to sacrifice her virginity to do her parents' bidding. Unlike
her, I would be able to keep my maidenhead intact. No
husband for me but the Heavenly Bridegroom for whom my
mother had yearned all those years, ever since that encounter
with the holy Fathers on the beach.

So I came to Ireland and the convent, my salvation. I was
welcomed into the community of devout women, marvelled at
as a prized gift of my mother's giving. My mother had
dedicated the most precious thing she had to the Lord: her
only child.

I learned to bend my head and move my lips as if in
constant prayer to escape the stares and the whispers.

I settled in. I'd always known that this would be my life. The
world at bay, I safe in the faith; six prayers a day from midnight
to midnight. Life rolled by. The seasons were the only thing
that changed. Every day brought us closer to the death of the
flesh, life eternal of the soul. Every time a sister died, we
celebrated the beginning of her life in the Lord.

It was a wandering preacher who brought me the news from
home. He was one of the men who travelled spreading the
faith, just like the ones who had met my mother on the bit of
sandy beach.

My mother was dead, had died with the name of the Lord
on her lips. It was my father who had killed her when he'd

heard that she had taken me away and would not tell him where I was.

The sisters came fluttering all around me, eager and envious.

'She is with the Lord!'

'How proud you must be.'

'She died a martyr for the faith.'

I got away in the end and went to kneel in the chapel, my lips moving automatically. They would have liked to talk more, but they could not interrupt my prayers.

What a waste, I thought. I wanted to cry but my eyes burned, dry as tinder. What a waste. Why should she die for believing in a different god? Why should she not tell my father where I was, and live? Buried in a convent or buried in a marriage, it was all the same to me. No one had asked me what I wanted.

It was as if the heavy shutters on the chapel windows had banged open and let fresh air and sunlight into the dark.

I had never known that I didn't like life in the convent. It would have been futile to think about what I did or did not want, because my thoughts counted for nothing.

But already it was too late. I knew now that I did not want to be where I was. I did not want to be a nun. I did not want to be a wife. I did not want my father's gods nor my mother's Lord. I wanted the freedom of fishermen: to come and go and work with my hands and my body, proud of my knowledge of the weather and the currents. I wanted the freedom of the convent's maids whom I'd seen at night, more than once, in the orchard; skirts hiked high and bodices undone, hands or mouths busy between each other's thighs. They didn't have to keep themselves pure for a husband or for the Lord. They weren't required to pray all day. The holy sisters had long given up their souls as lost, and anyway, they were only servants.

I tried to close the shutters in my mind that had so suddenly opened on thoughts I hadn't known were mine. I fastened them and turned my back on them and I began to pray in earnest, begging the Lord for forgiveness, praying for my mother's soul.

I ought not to grieve for her. She was in heaven, she was a holy martyr whom the Lord prized above all, she would sit at His right hand. I bowed my head, prayed six times a day for the salvation of my soul. I believed in the Lord.

Father Hugh had died. He had been old and frail, and for months had been unable to journey out to the far-away convent to take our confession and absolve us. We had been unshriven for a long time.

Father Diarmuid came instead. He was young and strong, and his beauty blazed like a bonfire. He moved as gracefully as a cat. His habit flowed loosely around him, but when a gust of wind moulded it against his body, I could see him as clearly as though he was wearing nothing at all. I knew that I wanted to do with him what the maids did in the orchard with each other.

I knew that it was wrong and impure. I would lose my maidenhead and my salvation. I was afraid of losing my eternal soul to damnation, but the wanting in my body was stronger. I was tired of being a virgin for the Lord.

I went to confession twice in two days, and when he heard my voice the second time, he opened the grille to look at me. I lifted my head and looked back at him, and said, 'Meet me in the orchard tonight'.

He was there. His beauty shone in the moonlight, he drew me like a magnet. The long grasses caressed my thighs as I walked towards him. And when my hand touched his naked skin, the shutters in my mind flew wide open and a gust of wind blew through me, so strong that it lifted me up and spun me around and made me fly.

Of course, they found us out in the end. We were caught one night in autumn when the cold rain had driven us indoors.

They beat him with birch rods until he bled and begged forgiveness. They made me watch. After they had birched me too, they held a council and decided that as I had come from across the sea to them – a stranger; not one of them as had become abundantly clear – I was to be put in a rudderless boat and sent where it pleased the Lord to take me.

When day broke, all I saw around me was water. Waves smacked against the sides of the boat. A wind rose and slapped me with raindrops, hard and cold.

The boat drifted on and on. I was going to drown or starve, and I did not care which it was going to be. Clouds moved across the sky all grey day long, until night fell again.

When the second day broke, I saw a dark line on the horizon. I was drifting towards it. Suddenly, I was certain that the land was my island, the place I came from, the place where my father lived and my mother had died. I was going to be washed up on the same piece of sandy beach where the Fathers had met my mother; I was being carried by the same current. I imagined my father's face as I arrived, and I had to laugh and laugh and couldn't stop.

The land came nearer. I could see the outline of a rocky coast, steep cliffs The laughing stopped, and instead I was afraid, terribly afraid. I was on my way back to my father's lands. He was going to kill me as he had killed my mother. I was a disobedient daughter and not a virgin any more.

I began to pray, gabbling with fear. I promised the Lord that I was going to be a faithful daughter; that I was going to keep myself chaste. I promised Him that I was going to beat the bad urges out of my body. The holy sisters had shown me how when they had beaten Father Diarmuid and me in the chapel after they caught us sinning. I suddenly understood that what we had done was a sin against the faith and the Lord, because it went against the laws that He had laid down. I understood that I was nothing and that the Lord was everything. I had been given to Him, I was His and no longer mine.

The land came nearer. There were jagged mountains on the horizon, blue as clouds. I was washed ashore at the foot of a steep cliff. This was not my island.

I was saved.

I fell on my knees in prayer to thank the Lord. Then I set about doing His work. I had to subdue my will and my unruly body. So I carried large stones up the steep cliff path, one after the other. I would build a church. Soon my hands were rough and bleeding, my back bent and aching. Every time I slipped and the stone rolled back down to the bottom and I had to start again, I fasted for penance. The winter storms lashed me with rain and hail. Some days I was so weak, I could not even lift a stone, let alone carry it up the cliff.

But every evening, no matter how tired and worn out I was, I used a birch rod to beat my body into submission. I had to keep my promise.

Every night, my lover visited me in my dreams. His hands stroked my wounds and scars and caressed my body until I swam in pleasure.

Every morning when I woke up, the wounds of the day before had closed and healed. Weeks passed, but nothing changed. The Lord would be displeased with me.

The birch was not enough.

I walked inland until I found a thorny shrub and tore off several of its branches. They would take care of the dreams.

But when the rods landed on my skin, their touch was as tender as a lover's fingers. They had grown white flowers whose sweet scent rose into my nostrils and made my head swim. The thorns had disappeared as though they had never been there.

I was going to burn in hell.

I ran down the cliff path and threw myself into the sea. There were sharp rocks just under the surface, impossible to evade. I braced myself for the shock of the cold, but the water was warm. It held me as though in a huge hand, blue and sparkling in the sunlight that had broken through the clouds.

The currents moved over my skin until my body uncurled all of its own accord.

I spent the next day collecting tufts of wool from the grazing sheep. I felt as though all the nuns in the convent were watching me, as well as the Lord; and I had to do something. When I had enough, I twisted the wool into thread. I knotted stones and broken shells with sharp edges into them until I had a formidable lash. I tried it out on the back of my hand. The threads wound round my fingers, curled and moved and hissed at my other hand when I tried to prise them loose.

The lash had turned into live snakes.

'Saint Patrick cast all snakes out of Ireland,' the voice of the Mother Superior said in my head. 'Snakes are the Serpent's foul brood. Saint Patrick was so pure that they could not abide him.'

Warm, dry bodies moved slowly over my skin, coiling and uncoiling, entwining themselves with my fingers. Tongues flickered as heads moved here and there.

They were beautiful.

Their beauty was like that of Father Diarmuid's body in the moonlight, like white blossoms against black wood, like air and sunshine through open windows.

I sat and looked at them and stroked their lovely, scaly bodies until, one by one, they unwound themselves from my hand and slipped away.

Then I got up and threw the birch rod off the cliff. It turned into a cormorant.

ollen

Sixth or seventh century

collen [f] – (n) hazel
Sometimes called *Collen Filwr*, Collen the
Warrior. A champion for Christianity, he
fought and killed a pagan warrior. Later
on, Collen became a wandering preacher
and missionary, settling down to live in
what is called today the valley of
Llangollen. At this time – according to
the legends – there was a cattle-stealing
and man-eating giantess living in the
area: *Cawres y Bwlch*, the Giantess of the
Pass. Collen decided to go and see her. As
he approached her cave and asked who
she was and what she was doing, the
giantess answered: *Myfi fy hun, yn fy
lladd fy hun.* (It is I myself, killing
myself.) He challenged her and they
fought. He sliced off her arm. She picked
up the bleeding limb and hit him with it.
He cut off her other arm as well and
eventually killed her.

According to a local version of this
legend, Collen was a woman.

1 was The Muscular Christian. My stage name, you see. *Wrestling for GOD.* For years and years of my life, I fought for God on a stage, not only for a living, but for a life.

'You've heard of Jacob wrestling the Angel! Who wants to wrestle with this angel here?' That always brought a roar of laughter from the crowds. I was fighting on the side of the angels, but I'm not exactly your fragile blonde. I'm six-foot-four in my socks and about three foot across and, as I say, I have a fair amount of muscle.

Now my mother was one of those fragile blondes. Me, I've got thick black hair that doesn't even curl. 'God only knows how you gave birth to that,' my stepfather used to say, and even when I was small I could tell that he didn't think I was a gift from heaven.

In the beginning she'd laugh and say, 'Well, her father was quite tall, I expect that's where she gets it from,' but after a while we both learned that he didn't like us mentioning my real Dad. He liked it even less when I said it that way. *My real Dad.*

'You're not my real Dad!' I'd scream at him when I was older, and then I'd run away and stay at a friend's for a night or two, until he'd simmered down. Two times out of three he'd have forgotten by the time I showed up again. Sometimes he didn't, and I got it with his belt. So I started the weight training. I'd pay him back one day, when I was stronger.

I expect that was why he hit me more, not less, as I got older and bigger. He wanted me to know that he was stronger.

'You're a freak!' he'd jeer. 'You'll never find a man!'

My mother had long given up saying anything by that stage. I just went on training every day, until every muscle in my body hurt. They did that often enough, anyway, so it didn't make much of a difference.

It was a sort of travelling circus that rescued me; Billy Graham meets Billy Smart, if you can imagine that. *Roll up, roll up and find the Lord!* Sounds daft, doesn't it, but it worked. I know, because that's how I found the Lord.

I was about sixteen when they came to our town, though I looked older.

Posters for GOD's Circus were plastered all over the place. It was a big spectacle in a place where nothing ever happened. Everybody was dying to go, although nobody admitted it. It was so tacky. But they all went, anyway. There was the tent with its flashing lights. Large banners announced the likes of *Samson, the Strongest Man on Earth, Lazarus Whom GOD Miraculously Raised From His Sickbed* (not from the dead, though) and *Mary Magdalen, The Sinner Who Repented And Found Life In GOD.*

Now I didn't much care for the repentant sinner, a miserable, wailing female – though I did notice that heads went up when she talked about her Life of Sin with a lot of unnecessary detail. After that, the preacher came on. His voice would have filled the big tent even without a microphone. Words flowed out of him like a river. He carried us all along in his current. Drops of sweat flew and glistened in the light. It was marvellous.

'And now, Ladies and Gentlemen!' he shouted. 'Let's see which of you are inspired by the Spirit of THE LORD!' The way he said GOD and THE LORD, you could hear that they were all made up of capital letters. The Virgin got just a capital initial. 'I give you Samson, the Strongest Man on Earth!'

On came a great lardy hulk of a man with a ruined nose and a shining bald skull. He looked like a prize fighter. It turned out he'd been a prize fighter – 'but then he found THE LORD! And now he fights in the corner of THE LORD! Gentlemen, which of you wants to chance a bout with the great Samson?'

Well, you know how it is. At first they're all shy. Girls look at their boyfriends from under their lashes. Mates elbow each other. Wives restrain husbands who couldn't wrestle open a marmalade jar. No one makes a move. God only knows what I thought I was doing.

I jumped up.

'I will!' I yelled. I thought it could be a sort of dress rehearsal. If I could beat this one, I was ready for my stepfather. The preacher wasn't sure what to make of me. 'Gentlemen!' he cried. 'Will you let yourselves be upstaged by a lady?'

Something came over me, and I'm not saying it wasn't the spirit of the Lord. 'Looks like it,' I said. That got me a few laughs.

By that time I was on the stage. I took off my jacket and handed it to the preacher.

'Right,' I said, rolling up my sleeves, flexing my muscles. The strongest man on earth looked on, not best pleased. He probably didn't like the idea of having to whack a girl in public.

He needn't have worried.

Lord, it was fun. We went for seven rounds, then I had him on the boards. It took him a bit longer than that to come round again.

The preacher did some quick thinking.

'Behold the Handmaid of THE LORD!' he roared, hauling up my hand. 'Behold, a miracle! David hath overcome Goliath!'

He offered me a contract that night, and Samson's job. 'A lady wrestler!' he said. 'That'll draw the crowds!'

It did. For the next eleven years, I fought for God.

The first six or seven of them, I even believed. God had seen me in my ungainly strength and taken mercy on me. He had seen my misery and found me a way out of it. He gave me a place in life where I could do His work and do what I did best.

I learned that there were others like me: girls who like men well enough, but who like other women better. I learned that not everybody thought I was a freak. I learned that some people thought all those muscles were really cool.

All was well with the world.

Then after a while, things wore thin. I'd had my miracle, but nothing else happened. I had articles written about me and my picture taken – *Hazel, The Strongest Lady on Earth!* – but nothing else *happened.*

Until one night, when the challenge to beat The Muscular Christian was taken up, for the first time, by another woman. You'd think there'd have been a few over the years, but no. By that time, I'd pretty much given up hope.

And then there she was, all glorious six-and-a-half foot of her.

We wrestled, Lord, how we wrestled! After the fight on the stage was over – which I had only just won – after my night on the stage was finally over and I could slip out and hope and pray to find her, we returned to our wrestling, in her bed.

The next day, I gave in my notice. As soon as I could, I returned to live with her. I settled down. I found work as a handywoman.

Life was good.

Then after a while, things wore thin.

I longed for my life on the road. I didn't like being tied down in one place. I missed the buzz of being on stage, the laughter and the cheers and the applause.

She wanted her freedom back. She missed going out with her mates. She said she missed being normal.

'What d'you mean, normal?' I said. 'At six foot six?' She hated being reminded of her height.

'You know what I mean,' she said. '*Normal.* As in going out with a bloke.'

Her mates had backed off pretty quickly when they'd found out that I wasn't just her new lodger. Good riddance to the silly, small-minded cows as far as I was concerned.

'I see,' I said. 'Time for that again, is it? I'm a pervert.

You're a straight woman who just happens to be sleeping with a lesbian. Shame the world can't see that.'

'Oh, shut up, Hazel!' she snapped. Last night one of her friends had cut us dead in the pub, and it still bothered her. 'Just face the flaming facts. You *aren't* bloody normal. Whatever normal is. Neither am I. So what? Why d'you want to be like everybody else?'

'Because we can't all be as grand as you. *The Strongest Woman on Earth!*'

'Oh, stop it!' I said, and gave her a playful push. She pushed me back. I put her in an arm lock. She bit my hand and rammed her elbow in under my ribs. I pinned her against the wall. She kissed me. I kissed her back.

We made love.

I enjoyed a good fight. So did she. It just bothered her that I was the stronger one. And it bothered her that she was taller than me. I'd always been looking for a woman I could look up to. So, presumably, had she. Correction. She had probably been looking for a man to look up to. Tough luck I came along.

She wanted us to stop going out together in public.

'I love you, Hazel,' she said, as we lay cuddled up in bed together. 'I really really do. But I've practically not seen any of my friends for months now! You know how it is... a small town... people talk.'

'I know how it is,' I said. 'I'm from one too. I live in one now. It's not a problem.'

'Well, it is for me,' she said shortly.

'Ashamed of me, are you? You stupid little bitch. Don't forget who you're insulting!' Eleven years of hearing myself called the strongest woman on earth had left their mark. I'd started to believe in it myself.

'Chosen by God, were you?' she jeered. 'Chosen to join his freak show!'

Nobody called me that. I hit her across the face. 'You stupid, big, lumbering giant!'

She flinched. I enjoyed that.

'Freak, freak!' she screamed. 'Was a stupid lumbering giant all you could find then? Would nobody else look at you?'

I pinned her arms down and started slapping her face. 'You,' I said, breathless, 'are nothing but a freak yourself.' Slap. 'And you're thick as well. Just look at you!' Slap. 'Six and a half foot tall, and you think if you hunch over a bit people will think you're little and delicate! You're big!' Slap. 'BIG!' Slap. 'Now, personally, I like big women, but as you just very helpfully pointed out, they're not everybody's cup of tea.'

She threw me off and knocked my head against the wall. 'Pervert! Freak!'

Something splintered somewhere. It might have been a piece of furniture, or her, or me. We didn't let it stop us.

'Let – me – go!' I gasped. Her arm was across my throat. I couldn't breathe. She was winning. I couldn't allow that. She wasn't the world's strongest woman. God was on my side, not hers. 'Let me go!'

She flew half-way across the room. Crashed into a couple of chairs. Slowly got up. Her mouth was bleeding, redder than lipstick.

She licked her lips, touched a finger to them. Grinned.

'Not bad, soldier,' she said, taking a couple of unsteady steps in my direction. 'Come and get me then.'

'You're mine,' I said, drawing a big red H on her like a cattle brand. It was only lipstick, but it looked real enough. '*Mine.* Remember that.'

She was trying on a new top in front of the mirror. She was going to go out with her mates. Without me.

'They'll come round eventually,' she said over her shoulder, adjusting a strap. 'Just give them time. They'll have to get used to it. I bloody have to get used to it myself!' She smiled at me.

'That looks really good on you,' I said.

'You think so?' Her smile got warmer.

'Mmm. Brings out your figure. Makes you look really slim. And tall.'

She tried not to flinch, but she did. She hated that word.

I liked putting the knife in like that.

'You bitch,' she said, her voice flat.

'Have a nice evening with those morons you call your friends,' I said. 'Maybe you'll pick up some really nice blokes. Oops. Sorry. Maybe *they'll* pick up some really nice blokes.'

She looked at me in the mirror. 'Maybe I'll pick up a nice bloke too. Thought of that?'

I hadn't.

'Sure,' I said. 'Be really nice for him to dance with his face in your cleavage. Such as it is. Be careful he doesn't stub his nose against your breastbone.'

She pretended not to hear, sprayed on some scent and was gone.

When she got back, I'd rearranged the bedroom.

What was left of the bed was burning in the living-room fireplace. What was left of the mirror was going to give somebody a lot of bad luck for some time to come. Her bad luck started when she walked into one of the splinters.

I was waiting for her behind the door. It was three in the morning.

'Had a nice evening?' I asked.

She whirled round. She had her new top on back to front. I ripped it off her.

She kicked my legs out from under me.

'Not only are you a loser,' she said clearly, 'but a bad one. You're leaving. I want you out of here by tomorrow.' And she turned round to leave.

Bad move. *Stupid* move. Did she think I was just going to

accept this? I grabbed hold of one of her legs and brought her crashing down next to me. I rolled over and pinned her to the floor with my weight.

'Did you get laid then?' I asked. 'Did you get fucked by a real man?'

She stared back. 'They find me attractive, you know. I may be a freak, but at least I'm not a pervert... '

You're a freak! You'll never find a man!

I had to shut her up. I couldn't let her get away with this.

That's why I'd done all the weight training and everything. So that nobody would call me those names ever again.

I had to show her.

I had to show her that I was the strongest woman on earth.

inifred

Sixth or seventh century

Also Winifrede, Gwenfrewi or Gwenffrwd.

Surprisingly, no records at all exist for this famous saint before the twelfth century, and her story bears striking parallels to elements in the *Vita* of a much older saint, which may well have been 'borrowed' in the later writing of Winifred's story. The healing well at Holywell was certainly well known and well visited since Roman times at least, but no particular legend appears to have been attached to it until the twelfth century.

According to the legend, Winifred was the daughter of Teuyth, a local chieftain and warlord, and his wife Gwenlo. Her maternal uncle was St Beuno, who taught her with a view to preparing her for life as a nun. One Sunday, when her parents were in chapel and Winifred alone at home, a local princeling came by and attempted to assault her. When she tricked him and managed to run away, he followed her in a rage and cut off her head. At the spot where her head fell, a spring bubbled up: St Winifred's Well. St Beuno then wrought a miracle and put her head back on her shoulders. Winifred chose to dedicate herself to a holy life.

1 suppose you could say I lost my head over him. That's what they're saying back home; only they twisted it all and now it's just lies and nothing else.

For a start, he wasn't rich or anything like that.

That was the problem.

And he never *ever* tried to rape me. I ran away with him.

ᴧᴧᴧ

My family didn't like Tariq very much.

Not only did he have wrong-coloured skin; but he's not even one of the New Middle Class. That's my Da's expression.

If he was one of the New Middle Class, now. They have very capable doctors and solicitors.

They. If *they* are diligent and hardworking, *they* can get to be *capable.* Not brilliant. Not composers, or painters, or Archbishops, or Prime Ministers. Or my boyfriend.

But Tariq isn't even like that. His Dad's a shopkeeper, you know, corner shop. He's even learned some Welsh and was in the local paper for it. And obviously Tariq and Aneesa learned Welsh in school, so between that and Urdu and English they're trilingual, really. They're *Welsh*, do you know what I mean? Born and bred here. When they went away to Leeds or London to visit their grandparents and aunties and uncles, they were homesick for the hills and the sea and the bilingual sign-posts. They struggled with Urdu and talked to each other in Welsh half the time.

Aneesa was my best friend, all the way from Year Four. I'd known Tariq as well, obviously, but only as Aneesa's brother, not, like, as a person.

Then one day I went back to her house for tea after school. It was during Ramadan and I'd fasted all day along with her. I was fourteen and very earnest. All my other friends had long since discovered boys and flirting and dancing and snogging, only I was still into books. I was a bit of a late starter. Aneesa was a little bit into boys and flirting, but she had also just discovered History. What she called 'our own history' – of where her parents had come from, Pakistan and India; and the Partition and the fight for Independence and stuff even before that. She said that suddenly her horizon had become dramatically bigger.

Aneesa is like that. Always off on a quest somewhere, being *inspired* by things.

Anyway, I hadn't really known about all the stuff she was talking about now; not really known, you know? Not like things that happened to real people like her Mum or her Dad. They'd just been things from the history books in school, or on the telly sometimes. Not *real*.

So I was sort of interested too, and thought I'd do a project about the Partition for history; it'd be dead easy really, I'd just have to follow Aneesa round for a bit and basically record everything she said, and then write that down properly and find a few pictures and stuff in the library, and there I'd be, project done.

So I went home with her that day for tea, and there was Tariq like I'd seen him dozens of times before, in the door to her room; I can still see him now, standing there and smiling at her and then at me and suddenly it was like I'd never really seen him before, like there was a spotlight trained on him so that I could see nothing else, only that smile and those eyes and what a beautiful neck he had and I thought, I want to be a vampire and bite him. And then Aneesa said something and I'd no idea what. I went beet red and mumbled something, and Tariq smiled again and went to his room, and I had to try to say something intelligent to Aneesa, and pretend my brain hadn't turned into a jellyfish.

Well, you know. I was in love, basically.

He was gorgeous, Tariq was. We went about holding hands a lot, and going off into the dunes and kissing and stuff, and it was great. I said, I don't want to do anything, you know, really really serious, not yet, and he was cool with that, and I think maybe he was relieved as well, because he'd not gone out with anyone before either.

I don't know why my parents were such ages finding out; I mean, it's not like we tried to hide anything. There wasn't anything *to* hide, if you know what I mean, we weren't *doing* anything, nothing really really serious; not like Karen in my class who got pregnant and had to leave before her GCSEs. I didn't want that, I wanted to go on to college or maybe university and do something with my life, you know, and so did he, we had time; we could wait.

And I'd got some condoms out of a machine, just in case.

Funny, really, because I thought I was being grown up and sensible. I'd got them just in case, because sometimes I thought, I don't really want to wait, I want to, you know, *do it*, like, now! Because what we were doing felt so good. And if we did, it'd be better to have something handy. But my Mum found them in my jeans pocket when she turned them out for the wash, although I'd asked her not to do that anymore, I thought I was old enough to do my own clothes, you know. But she said she'd had a machine nearly full, and was looking for something to put in it to fill it up, and so she just went through my clothes which were on the floor anyway, she said, as though that was a reason. And she said it just went to show that obviously I *had* things to hide and that was why I didn't want her to go through them, which was *not true*.

Anyway, I came home that evening and there were the condoms, on my plate at the tea table, if you please. And Mum and Da with faces like thunder, demanding an explanation. So I told them the truth.

I thought they'd praise me for my forethought.

Did they, hell! They set up a lament about how I obviously didn't trust them enough to come and talk to them and get advice before embarking on such a big step. (The word 'sex' wasn't mentioned *once*.)

I said we hadn't really embarked on anything yet, and that I didn't see why I should get advice if we weren't doing anything. Or even if we did.

I can see that that was a tactical error now, but at the time I was just really peed off that they were behaving like I was a little kid, when I'd been acting really sensibly and responsibly and everything.

I said, 'You *knew* I was going out with Tariq, we've been going out for ages!'

And my Da said that as far as he and Mum knew that had only been a kids' thing, only because I was friends with Aneesa. And how were they supposed to know if I didn't tell them?

'Well, excuse me,' I said, 'if I've been going out with a boy for almost two years and haven't said anything about having split up, then obviously I'm still going out with him, right?'

Wrong. It was only much later that I thought, maybe Mum and Da didn't *want* to know, maybe they didn't *want* to take Tariq and me seriously because they were hoping I'd grow out of him or something?

I mean, excuse me. I thought they were the adults. Adults are supposed to be mature, innit. You'd think I'd come home and told them I was *pregnant*, the way they carried on. And then it slowly came out that they weren't only peed off about the condoms and me growing up and all, but about who I was going to use them with, if you know what I mean. That's when my Da said that stupid sentence.

'We've got nothing against Tariq,' he said – and that was obviously not true anyway. 'We've got nothing against Tariq, but we must think about your future.'

I really wanted to point out that I *had* thought about the future, that that was why I'd bought the flaming rubbers, but

I'm not completely stupid and I reckoned it wasn't a good time to say that just then.

So my Da went on, 'If he was one of the New Middle Class, now. They have very capable doctors and solicitors.'

I didn't even get it at first. 'Who,' I said. '*They?*'

'People like Tariq's father and mother,' my Da said without blushing. My Mum looked uncomfortable.

'You mustn't think that we've got anything against them!' she said.

I still didn't get it. 'Why should you?' I asked, and she went red and pressed her lips together.

'What've Tariq's Mum and Dad got to do with it, anyway?' I said. 'I mean, it's not like we're going to get *married* or anything. I mean, not for ages, anyway.'

'I should think not,' my Da said, and that's when I finally clicked.

'But we might,' I said – to see if I was right.

'That's exactly what your mother and I are worried about,' my Da said pompously. 'You're far too young to make that sort of decision. You've no idea what a marriage with somebody from this sort of... um... background will mean.'

'What background?' I asked, all innocent.

'You know perfectly well what I mean!' he said, getting annoyed.

'Yes,' I said. 'You're a flaming racist, that's what! You want to tell me that I can't go out with Tariq because he's Asian. You don't want us to stay together and maybe get married and have kids because then your precious grandchildren would be mixed race and Muslim. You probably think Tariq and Aneesa and their Mum and Dad are *terrorists* because they're Muslims!'

I was screaming by then, I was *so* furious!

'I think that's really disgusting and small-minded of you,' I said, and I said that on purpose because my Da was always going round saying how open-minded we were in our house, and not like other people; and how we always travelled abroad and broadened our minds and stuff, and were really clever and progressive. So I said, 'That's really small-minded of you' – because it *was*.

And I said, 'And we haven't flaming *done* anything yet anyway, but you don't believe me, do you, you don't *trust* me! You've such filthy minds and you're stupid racists, you're not thinking about my future at all, are you, you're thinking about what the neighbours will say, and Gran and Taid! And I'm ashamed that you're my parents, I wish Mr and Mrs Ahmed were my parents!'

And then I ran out of the house like a little kid, and banged the door and went on a bus and went to the beach. I always go to the sea when I'm upset or worried or happy.

When Tariq and I first got together I had to go on a three hour walk along the sea front because I was so happy. We had our first kiss there as well, in the dunes. It was really romantic even though it's such a touristy place and we were knee deep in fish-and-chip wrappers and stuff; it was still great, and he tasted really, really wonderful with the sea salt on his lips.

I was thinking of that as I sat on the bus on the way down to the sea front, and I started to cry. I was in such a rage, and I thought of how happy we were together, Tariq and me, and how Mum and Da didn't see that at all, how it didn't matter to them.

And then I thought, All right, if they don't want me like that, then I'm moving out. It wasn't just the thing with the condoms, and how they talked about Tariq. There'd been other things as well. Like that time when they'd stopped me going to the cinema with my mates because it was two days before my fifteenth birthday, and we wanted to see a Certificate 15 film, and my Da had rung up the cinema and told them that his underage daughter was trying to get into that film, and they stopped me going in! It was just, like, so humiliating! So anyway, there I sat on that bus, thinking about all that stuff, and suddenly I thought: I can't stand this one more day. I'm moving out.

And, you know, I was thinking at the back of my mind that I'd only move out as a sort of warning. Or to show Mum and Da that I was almost grown up, and that I was a real person, an almost-adult person who could make her own decisions, and that I wanted to be treated like an adult, you know?

I stomped up and down the sea front, and then I went really close to the sea, and it was a windy day and really big, noisy waves, and I went and screamed and screamed into the waves until I was all hoarse. But afterwards I felt better.

I rang Tariq on my mobile and told him what had happened, and that I had decided to move out. He was worried at first, and said, 'What are you going to live on?' But I said I'd thought about that, and I would get a job and stuff, work in a call-centre or whatever, and that I thought anyway it would only be for a bit, until my parents saw that we were serious.

He wasn't really sure at first, but then we met up and we talked it all through, and slowly he was beginning to like the idea as well.

So anyway, that's what we did. We found this little flat, and I thought I'd probably have to work the checkouts at Kwik Save, but I was really lucky and got this job in an office; not great but it paid for my half of the rent and stuff, and I loved the independence.

Mum and Da didn't believe it at first when I told them what I was going to do, and that I was moving in with Tariq. I thought they'd take me more seriously, but instead they started yelling and screaming at me, and then they said they were going to stop me because I was too young, and it was against the law and they'd get an injunction or something and go to court – I mean, I couldn't believe it. I thought we'd sit down and talk.

And they just never came round.

It's been more than a year now and they're not even talking to me. I mean, I still try to ring them from time to time but they just put the phone down when they hear my voice, even Mum.

I don't know why. It makes me really sad, and even Tariq can't always help. How can they be like that?

We moved to Liverpool, Tariq and me, a few weeks ago, because it was just getting too difficult back home. His parents are sort of OK about us – well, I mean, they did have forty fits, but they'd never throw Tariq out, you know what I mean? And they didn't call me names, ever. And Aneesa's really great and supportive and everything, but it was doing me in having to walk past my house in the street and knowing I couldn't go there. I tried, but my parents were just really icy and said they didn't think we'd have anything to talk about. I'd made my bed and now I must lie in it, and it wasn't any good coming to them for help. That just set me off again and I screamed at them until they closed the door in my face.

Shit.

Aneesa is still living at home, and since I've got the new job here and she got her new computer, we've been on the email all the time.

She wrote to me about the stories my parents have been telling people. They're saying that I moved away because of the strain. That I was attacked and assaulted and that I had a nervous breakdown and have gone away to my aunt and uncle's to recover. And the really weird thing, Aneesa writes, is that hardly anybody says, 'But didn't she move in with her boyfriend? Didn't she have this job in an office?' It's as if they've forgotten. It's only been a few months, and already this legend of my parents is stronger than reality.

But it can't last. Can it?

Non

The daughter of a provincial petty king or chieftain, Non was probably a nun. She was raped by the King of Ceredigion. When she fell pregnant she herself was blamed for this sign of what was deemed her 'sexual incontinence', and excluded from the convent.

She left to live in a hut near the cliffs at Bryn y Garn (today St Non's Bay), where she gave birth during a raging tempest. During labour, she is said to have pressed her fingers into a nearby rock with such force that the marks are still visible.

She later founded convents in Wales and Cornwall, as well as in Brittany, where she is said to be held in higher regard than even her famous son, St David.

1 used to be able to fly.

I would fly to work, but then people started commenting on how I climbed in through the window every morning. I took it as a compliment at first, but after I'd been taken aside a couple of times by motherly types and given gentle hints about what they called my 'oddity', and how this wouldn't do my career any good, I decided to land in the park across the street and walk up the stairs like, apparently, everybody else.

I thought they all flew. I assumed they just didn't let on during the working day, reserving it for after hours, when they'd hover in the garden over their roses, bobbing on the breeze and enjoying the scent.

But they thought that I was odd.

I think they're afraid They even strap their children down in their buggies so that they don't lift off where people can see.

I wanted to have a career, so I adapted and began to walk in public as well. I tended to do the flying only when nobody was watching. My manager knew, but he didn't seem to mind.

We usually went out on a Friday night, whoever was still in the office at the time; it was that sort of place. Sometimes it was just the manager and me, but he always behaved OK. I could talk to him intelligently, which isn't something you often find in a boss.

Only one evening it ended differently.

I still can't remember all of it. I remember the lights in the bar; strobe lights, so it must have been a club, and it was late. I remember drinking a bit but not being drunk and the police confirmed that; I was well under the limit for driving. Only I didn't drive; he gave me a lift home and I didn't see why not; it was the middle of January, sleeting and raining. 'You won't have much fun flying home in that,' he said and I agreed. 'Save you the cab fare.'

I accepted, he'd done it before when the weather was bad, and I knew him for a safe driver; I would never have thought it of him. Then we're in his car and he's driving not to my house but somewhere else, and I'm surprised, and there's his hand on my thigh and I'm confused and from then on it doesn't make sense.

I remember a face above me. Breathing.

I remember feeling surprised, disbelieving. There are hands on me. His hands. They find their way under my clothes although I'm struggling. They slap me across the face when I say No.

Then it's dark. And cold.

Cold.

I don't know where I am.

There is no pain.

Yet.

All I feel is cold.

So cold.

I'm dead. I can see myself lying huddled on the ground. I can see the man getting up. I know there is a man but I've forgotten who he is. I know something has happened just now but I've forgotten what it was.

The man is breathing heavily. He tidies himself up, straightens his clothes. He does not look at me.

He tells me to get up and back into the car.

He drives me home.

He opens the car door and waits until I get out and kisses me on the cheek and says goodnight.

I walk up to my front door and hear him drive away. I am tired and my legs are unsteady so I sit down on my doorstep.

Then there is a long time of nothing.

A pain pierces through the deadness and something pulls

me, pulls me like a current. Smell hits me. A wall of sound. I sit still while everything roars around me.

Much later, there is a light in my eyes. I am being taken to hospital, examined, having samples taken from me before I am allowed to wash. I do not know who I am. I do not know what has happened. They tell me I rang 999 on my mobile after it happened (after what happened? Everybody just says 'it'), that I rang the police and an ambulance and screamed and raged, but I can't remember anything of that.

For weeks afterwards, everything is grey. I have become an old woman, weak and breathless, barely alive. I shrink from light, from noise, from touch, from life around me.

I cannot fly any more.

I want to die. For a long time, I want to die, but I don't.

I don't and I don't and I don't. I am enraged that I am still alive. I roam the rooms of my house. I can't settle down to anything. I scream. I wail. I hurl glasses and plates against the walls. I cry and howl and yell. I break planks of wood against door frames, slam the windows and break their glass panes.

One day, I slam the front door behind me and see a large crack appearing right across it.

Splinters of memory are coming back. A streetlight. The yap of a small dog in the distance. The scream of an ambulance. Music through an open car window, too loud for anyone to hear my voice over it. The look on the face above me. The mouth opening, a voice issuing, telling me to be quiet. Telling me that I wanted this. Telling me where to put my hands, ordering me to smile, to say that this is good.

Despair like a dead thing inside me. Craven fear and shame and helplessness.

I wonder why nobody asked me if I wanted to press charges. In fact, a solicitor advised me against it. It would be my word against the man's, the solicitor said, and the conviction rate in these cases was very low. According to the man, it was consensual sex, he said. According to the man, I liked a little rough and tumble. I did not have any witnesses, he said. I had been out with the man and I did not really have a case, he said.

I was too numb to say anything.

I wonder why nobody shoved a knife into my hand and urged me to cut the bastard into strips, for my greater good and that of the community.

I know who he is, the man who violated me.

I know where he lives, so I go there to watch him, and to follow him when he is next going to venture out alone.

I am going to have my revenge.

A tooth for a tooth. An I for an I. He has killed the best part of me. So now I will do the same for him. A death for a life. My life.

But when I see him, the breathlessness comes back. I cower in the shadows, hiding myself, afraid of what he will do if he sees me. The pain echoes through my body, as though the body was a thing separate from me with its own memory. I can do nothing but stand there, helpless, and watch him move off out of sight.

I hate myself.

I have no courage. I will not dare go back and try again.

I have failed. He is stronger. I am weak, I am nothing.

I go home, and see the crack across my front door. I am furious with myself for having run away. I slam the door shut behind me, and a large piece of plaster falls from the ceiling. I kick the skirting-board, and there is a hole in the wall.

Next morning I am on my watch again.

I am still surprised by the fear that crashes over me like a wave when I see him. I am breathless, and wet with sweat. I follow him on unsteady feet. My hands shake. I feel sick and small and weak. I follow him. He turns round once, his eyes sweeping over me as if he is looking for someone, something.

He does not even recognise me. I am nothing to him. I shake again, but this time it is with anger.

I will make him remember.

I wait until the time comes for my next bleeding, and then I spend almost a whole day taking off my clothes and stuffing them between my thighs, until everything is covered in red stains.

When evening comes, I look for him. I find him at home, by himself, which is lucky. He is sitting out on the terrace. I tear the lock out of his front door and go inside.

At the sound of my footsteps he looks up. 'Who is that?' he asks, squinting into the shade.

I say my name in a voice that comes out weak and breathless, and he smiles. He smiles at me. At me.

'Well, hello there,' he says. His voice is hearty. 'I haven't seen you for ages! Not since...' He reflects. 'Not since our little outing, in fact.' He still smiles.

I feel as though I have been slapped. Again. I cannot find my voice.

I only move out onto the terrace because that's what I had planned to do. I cannot think. I want to run away. I feel like I have been given a second chance, the chance to run away, but I am too stunned to do anything except move out onto the terrace because that's what I'd planned to do.

I speak the words I have thought out beforehand. I speak like an automaton.

'Do you remember me? Do you remember what you did to me? Look what you have done to me!'

He looks up.

He sees my bloodstained clothes. His smile slips.

I put my hand between my legs and dip it in and spray him with the blood.

He recoils.

Now I smile.

I lean against the door frame and cross my arms over my chest.

'Do you remember me?' I say. 'Remember the ride in the car? How I asked you to take your hand away? How I asked you to stop? How I screamed because it hurt? How you put your hands around my neck and squeezed. *Remember?*'

I can see from his eyes that he does remember, now. He tries to put his smile back into place.

'I thought you enjoyed that,' he says.

I cannot breathe. I remember the hands round my neck. I move forward and, before he has time to react, I slip a rope round his neck. I pull it tight. My hands feel alive. I am rewarded with the astonished look on his face that is now becoming red, and the sound of his breath whistling in gasps.

But then the moment of surprise is over, and he lifts his hands and puts them between my arms, and he shoves my arms apart, and I remember how much stronger than me he was that night, and I remember the fear and how I couldn't breathe, and my arms drop and the rope falls from his neck and we stand there, chest to chest on his terrace; and I want to run away.

I bend down and pick up the rope and he doesn't stop me. And then I turn around and walk away. And he doesn't stop me.

At home, I smash every plate and glass and mug in the house. I rage and scream and fling myself against the walls after the crockery has run out.

Then I sit in the silent house and listen to the small bright sound of glass splinters settling.

I need a break. I take a weekend off and spend it by the sea. Pebbles are a good start, but they soon become too small, sailing lazily through the air and dropping into the water with an elegant little splash.

There are some boulders further up the shore. I try to lift a small one and find that I can do it quite easily. But when I throw it, it falls far short of where I have aimed it, just a few feet away from where I am standing. I get drenched.

I think of the ride in the car. I think of myself stupefied with shock, with disbelief; weighed down so that I cannot fly away. I think of myself now, unable to fly.

Filled with fury, I pick up another large rock and hurl it with as much strength as I have. It flies in a beautiful arc, for quite a long time, then disappears into the sea. I can see white foaming up where it falls, but I don't hear the splash. I bend down for the next one.

By the evening of that day, I can heave up a boulder as large as myself and throw it a good few yards.

By the end of the weekend, I can throw one of those boulders so far that I don't hear the splash as it hits the water.

I leave the beach and walk inland, juggling with some rocks as large as my head. I go back to the house of the man who has violated me. I can see that he is at home, because his car is parked outside. I remember the car. It is the same one that he gave me the lift in. I throw the rocks at it. They bounce off the metal, only leaving some dents. The car alarm starts to wail. I pick up the car; I am surprised how light it is. I toss it from hand to hand, then throw it against the garage wall. There is a loud bang and a crash and dust billowing, and then the house alarm goes off as well.

I kick down the front door of the house and go inside.

I meet the man in the corridor; he has heard the crash and the alarms and I can see that they have done their job. He is alarmed.

He is even more alarmed when he sees me. I am pleased.

He tries to move past me, but I block his way.

'Let me through,' he says.

'No,' I say. Oh, what a lovely feeling this is, to say No and stretch out my arms to block his passage, and to see him stop.

Not for long though; he still tries to squeeze past.

I pick up a small hall table and hurl it at the ceiling. Splintered wood and lumps of plaster rain down on us. His eyes open wide, he backs away. I tread on his toes, step by step, and force him onto the terrace.

'What do you want?' he asks. He really does not know.

'You know who I am?' I want to make certain.

'Yes,' he says, testily.

'You know what you did?'

Silence.

I kick his shin and repeat the question.

'Yes!' – as though I had reminded him of something he'd rather not remember. I suppose I have.

'You owe me an apology. I want you to say that you're sorry.'

He gapes.

I find that I am screaming at him. 'Do you *know* what you have done?! Do you have any idea what it felt like? What I felt like? You shit!!' I kick his shin again, and his crotch, hard; I pick him up and slam him against the garden fence.

Neighbours' startled faces appear and quickly duck out of sight again.

I grab him by his shirt collar and swing his body through the air; then I let go. I see him fly and am reminded that I may now be forever earthbound, because of what he has done to me.

I scream and I roar. I pluck him out of the air and send him flying again with a punch, like a volleyball, like a football, again and again and again.

Finally, out of breath, I drop him into his rose bush from a great height and look down on him as he crawls, slowly and painfully, out of it. I haven't felt this good for a long time.

Then it strikes me what I am doing. I am looking down on him. I am in the air and he is on the ground.

I leave him to his crawling.

I fly to the nearest B&Q and pick up a couple of bags of cement and plaster and a new door.

And then I fly home.

ydfil

Fifth century

Tydfil (also Tudful or Tudvul) was one of the many daughters and sons of King Brychan. She was killed in about the year 480 by a band of marauding pagans, either Saxons or Picts. Much is known about Tydfil's death and the manner in which her brother Rhun avenged it, but almost nothing appears to have been written about her life.

The town of Merthyr Tydfil is named after her.

Do you know what *Merthyr* means?

It means Martyr.

Do you know what *Martyr* means?

It means Witness.

Listen.

What do you hear?

The breath of the wind. The calls of jackdaws, ravens, magpies. The songs of thrush and blackbird. The laughter of the river as it trips and hurries over stones, towards the sea, towards the sea.

At night, the river tells me stories of the sea, of the huge inky wateriness of the ocean that is the dream of every little spring and brook. Soon, soon, the waters sigh as they slide past me. Soon, the sea.

I have never wanted anything but this: my river, my valley, my forest full of ancient trees and many creatures, and my own company. Occasionally also Brother Pedr's but, praise be, he never stays long. Brother Pedr comes by every month to hear my confession and have me hear his so that we can absolve each other. He is a hermit like me. He lives more than half a day's walk away to the south, in a cave on a hillside. Before he became a hermit, he swore many solemn oaths: to give up the pleasures of the world and the flesh and all human company and to chastise himself in solitude. When he found me living in my hut by the river one day, he made me swear the same oaths.

He would not have understood that what was a sacrifice to him was for me the lifting of a stone from my heart. What could there be in the world that was better than this?

He left children and a wife whom he still misses keenly, but he loves God more than he loves them.

I left behind a local warlord who fancied me for a wife, and a father and mother who couldn't believe their luck that somebody would take me off their hands. I did not give up a life like Brother Pedr. I found one here, far away from those of my own kind.

ᕕᕗᕕ

Listen.

There is the sound of horses' hooves on the wind, the clink of metal on metal, the creaking of saddle leather.

There are men coming this way.

I try to hide but it is too late. I run, but not fast enough.

Look.

There is my body on the ground, a knife in my side in the very place where Jesus was pierced by the soldier's lance when he hung on the cross. Brother Pedr would be pleased by the sight. He sets great store by the sufferings of Our Lord, and of those of the holy martyrs and confessors who died at the hand of the Ungodly. But I am not pleased. I cannot tear myself away from the memory of the pain, from the sight of the blood that streams out of my body.

The men who have just killed me are now tearing down the hut that I call my church; it is only made out of wood, with clay to stop the leaks in the walls and roof. A moment later it is just a heap of firewood. I hear the crackling of the flames and even feel the heat. I want to cry. This was my house, I built it with my own hands.

I wait. I wait until, finally, they leave. Then I sit by the river for a long time until all I can hear is silence again. But the stink of burning and of blood will not leave my nostrils.

I drift away, along the stream, into the hills and the trees. I will live here where killings occur only out of necessity, because a fox and a bear must eat, not because they're greedy for power or gold.

I stay with the trees and the birds and the shrews and the foxes for a long time. I spend days and weeks watching the pattern of light and shadow change on the hills, listening to the hiss and whisper of the rain. I spend a lifetime inside a tree, slowly growing and stretching with it; feeling leaves and acorns drop from me in autumn, feeling the storms tug at my branches and bending with them in a wild dance; feeling new leaves bursting out of my fingertips every spring.

One autumn, many seasons later, the tree, grown old and heavy with life, is toppled by a storm, and I have to look for a new home.

I tell myself that I am now, after all, ready to leave this world and move on to the next. I have grown many, many years older than anybody I knew when I was still alive. But my hunger for life has not lessened.

For the first time since I have come to live in the forest, I wonder what has happened to the place where I used to live. Brother Pedr must long since have died, but another might have taken his place. Or mine.

I decide to go and have a look. It is a long time since I saw one of my own kind.

There is a little hamlet now by the river, with my church rebuilt in the place where it used to be, and a stone cross beside it.

A group of women are busy by the river, some washing clothes in the water while others wring out the heavy wet bundles and others still spread them out to dry over bushes and on the short, hard grass to the left and right of them. Children herd goats and pigs and geese on the Green.

I go into the church. I have missed it.

A girl is kneeling in front of the cross on the altar, just in the place where I used to kneel. How I envy her her life.

She is praying silently. Then she looks up and for a

wonderful moment I think she can see me. Has she heard me?
Seen me? Felt my presence?

Am I a ghost now?

She is crying. 'Help me please, Father. In the name of Saint
Tydfil... ' It seems I have become a saint in my absence.

'I wish I could help you,' I say.

She is turning her head, as if she has heard a sound and
does not know where it might have come from.

'Tell me,' I say, speaking slowly and clearly, as though that
could make her hear me. 'Tell me.'

Words and tears spill out of her. She is an orphan and a
servant to anyone who needs work done and will give her food
and a place to sleep in exchange. Her name is *You little slut
there,* but she likes to call herself Morfudd. She has just spent
a week looking after the house and children of Mair who had
her eighth lying-in, and now she has been accused of stealing
Mair's good sewing needle.

'I didn't take it, as God is my witness!' she says, although she
can hardly speak for being convulsed with sobs. 'I did not, I did
not, but they don't believe me, they're going to take me before
the court, and Mair says I'm going to have my th- thieving hand
cut off!' She is terribly frightened. I think if she had taken the
needle, she would not still be here.

'I wish I could help you,' I say again, and I stroke her bent
head and say her name, 'Morfudd, Morfudd,' to let her know
that to me at least, she is not a slut.

As she becomes a little calmer, I put my lips to her ear and
whisper, 'I will help you.' She crosses herself and says the
Lord's Prayer. Then she looks around to make sure that
nobody sees her, and kisses the crude little wooden doll to the
side of the altar that is supposed to be me although I never had
long golden hair in my life.

When she slips out of the church, I follow. We go to a house
on the other side of the Green. Morfudd creeps in on tiptoes,
clearly hoping not to be noticed.

From a bed in the corner a woman props herself up on her elbows and begins to scream at her. Morfudd does not try to defend herself, she merely stands, shoulders sagging, and waits until it is over. This infuriates the woman even more. She scrabbles around on the floor near her and throws something. The pisspot, as it happens. Several small children begin to wail. Chickens scatter in alarm. The straw wall drips.

'Out!' yells Mair. 'Out, you daughter of sin, you ungrateful harlot!'

Morfudd flees.

I advance upon the woman on the bed. 'How dare you,' I say. 'The wrath of God upon you! Have you no heart? What is a needle but dead metal... '

She rises and marches through me. She does not see me; she has not heard one word I said. She goes to a corner of the house, impatiently chases away a scratching chicken, and digs in the straw. Something glints in the thin sunlight that comes in through a chink in the wall.

A needle.

Mair coos over it, laughs, and puts it away again carefully. She straightens up.

'Slut,' she says in the direction of the door through which Morfudd has run. And spits on the floor.

I spend all afternoon jumping into her path and telling her what a sin she is committing in treating poor Morfudd like this, lying and telling falsehoods. But she does not see or hear me at all. To her, I am not even a ghost.

As evening comes, I want nothing so much as to return to my forest, to the quiet, the absence of human voices, human greed, human malice. I am tired of my own kind.

I start to leave, to go back to the trees, but as I pass my church I remember Morfudd there this morning, praying to God in my name, sobbing with fear and despair.

I will try one more thing. I go back to Mair's house and I sit down in a corner with the chickens and the ducks.

I ask them to help me. Together, we hatch out a plan.

As a couple of Mair's neighbours come to see her and the newborn later on, the fowl show an unusual interest in this one particular corner. They scratch and scrabble and finally set up a noisy chorus of cackling and quacking. The women come to look, and are confronted with the sight of one hen with the missing needle in her beak, while another flutters to sit on Mair's bed and shouts – with a little help from me – 'She took it, she hid it! She took it, she hid it!'

The Day the Chickens Spoke in Tongues will be remembered in the village for generations. Morfudd keeps both her hands. She stays in the village for a few months more – visiting the church every day – then she decides that she wants to see the world. So she goes to the market town across the hill, half a day's walk away. She walks right across the hill, past the gibbet outside the town wall, through the open gate and into the town that is full to bursting with people: more than she has ever seen in her life. It is a large town and she is frightened; there are cripples and beggars at every corner and they chase her away; they do not want her for competition. So Morfudd knocks on doors, asking for work.

After the first week, she is ready to give up and go back.

At the end of the second, she has a post: a woodcarver requires a servant in his household and takes her on.

When some years later his wife dies, Master Mihangel marries his maid-of-all-work, causing no little stir. But he doesn't care, and neither does Morfudd. She makes a good wife and help-meet who quickly learns Mihangel's craft from him. After his death, she keeps the shop open, just like her friend Heledd, the apothecary's wife, had done some years previously, after her husband died. She becomes Mistress Morfudd, the woodcarver.

One day, she is asked to supply a saint's statue for a new church they're building in her home village. The priest wants a

Martyred Tydfil with pink cheeks and golden hair and a lot of arrows sticking out of her.

But Mistress Morfudd makes a different statue: a short woman with dark hair and a smile on her lips.

She walks across the mountains and puts it up in the church herself; she tells people that she is making a pilgrimage. The new church is built of stone: much grander than my little hut ever was. Morfudd hesitates for a moment before crossing its threshold; then she enters slowly and puts the statue down. She looks around herself, uncertain.

'I don't know if you're still here. I wanted to thank you.'

I give her a kiss on the ear for an answer, and she smiles and kisses the statue back.

For a time I live in my new church, inside Morfudd's statue. I listen to people's wishes and prayers and help where I can. Girls tell me about their troubles and ask for painless monthly bleedings, deliverance from an unwanted marriage, happiness in love. Some seek mercy from a mother who torments them with beatings or a father who uses them as he would a wife.

A new priest comes to the village, and soon my ears are full of stories from children who cry while they tell me of his wandering hands and the cruel pinchings he gives them in parts of their bodies he calls dirty and sinful.

I take myself off into the forest to ask the help of some of the creatures there. I feel a great weight lifting as I am back on the hillside, in the changing light made by the patterns of wandering clouds, in the sighing winds and the gold and brown and green of leaves and branches. When I return to the village, I am not alone. I bring with me a plague of wood lice to infest the priest's house, woodpeckers to drum on his walls and shutters during the day and owls to keep him awake at night.

Every time he goes out, I walk beside him and shout, 'Confess your sins!' in his ear, until I feel like a *gwdihw* myself.

Before the old moon has quite changed into the new, the priest has left.

The wood lice, owls and woodpeckers go back to the forest and the hills, and I decide to go with them. I have seen enough of my own kind.

ᴧᴧᴧ

I share the bodies of birds for many generations. The feel of the wind through my wing feathers is so like the breeze in my leaves when I was a tree; but oh, the ecstasy of flying; the exhilaration of tussles won against the wind; of plummeting down, down, down like a stone with the air screaming in my ears, only to open my wings at the last moment and to sail upwards again, up and up and up until all the world is sky and cloud, cold air and gusting wind and the earth far, far below.

I do not think that I will want to go back to the world of my own kind, not yet, not for a long time, perhaps not ever again. But one day, they start coming into my forest on the hillside.

First it is groups of women and children, collecting bundles of wood. Then it is men with axes and saws. They start cutting down the trees.

From the valley below, columns of smoke rise, clouds of burning sparks explode. They are burning my trees.

In the place of the hamlet now stands a town. There is a forest of buildings made of stone. The earth has been studded with stones and covered with ashes and filth, animal dung and human shit. The smell of smoke is everywhere. There is a neverending thudding and screeching and the roar of human voices, day and night. My ears hurt. I have never seen so many people in one place. Even Morfudd's market town across the hills was not as large as this.

After a time, my ears attune themselves to the constant noise. I begin to pick out individual voices. There are many people who speak a language I don't understand. Others speak my language, but with accents I have never heard before.

I look for my church and finally find it. It is still in its old place, but it is now hemmed in by houses on every side, and it has changed yet again. It has become a dark, solemn building. I go inside. Morfudd's statue is gone.

But I suppose it is still my church.

I listen to the prayers of the people who come in. Many girls speak of homesickness for the fields and hills they have left behind in order to come to this grey, stinking place.

I sit by them and whisper stories in their ears of life as a tree, as a bird, as an ant, as a fish in a stream, as a bear in the forest. I talk of the currents of wind and water, of brown soil teeming with creatures. I tell them what it feels like to move as a many-legged wood louse, as a teetering spider, as a slick, slithering earthworm. They listen, and when they leave their backs seem straighter, their faces a little less pale.

Most of them are servants, like my Morfudd before she became Mistress Morfudd the woodcarver. They have come to work in this grey place with its shroud of smoke because they were looking for work, for money, for food. I follow them when they leave my church. I watch as they work: one lifts heavy sheets out of tubs of steaming water, another serves pints of ale, a third has sex with men down dark alleys. They sew clothes, cook meals, break up lumps of stone with heavy hammers, pick pockets, run errands for a mistress.

The barmaid is Siân. Elizabeth is a widow, a seamstress who takes in laundry. When there is no work and no food for her children, she walks the streets for a week, for a month, until times get better. Mary works in one of the mines that burrow deep underground to bring up stone that burns with a fierce heat. Gwen and Bess are servants in the house of a magistrate who sometimes uses the services of Jennie the whore. His wife knows, and takes her shame and anger out on Bess and Gwen.

And yet Jennie and Siân, Sara and Mary, Elizabeth and

even Gwen come to my church to listen to my stories of life in the forest, yes, but also to give thanks to God for having led them to this town. Life here is hard, but life at home was impossible. There is food here. Money. Freedom. At home, they might have starved. They would not have found a husband, or would have been married against their will. So they left. Some ran away. Here, there is a chance of seeing the world. Adventure. Riches even! says Jennie and they laugh.

I am envious of the lives of those girls. I ran away from home, once, when I was still alive.

I have been dead for so long.

They have left my church, all except for Sara, the pickpocket. She is very young, not yet fifteen, and has nowhere to live. She has come a long way, and sometimes she still looks over her shoulder to make sure that nobody is following her. She has run away from the stick in her mother's hand. She has not been here long enough for all the scars on her body to fade from the colour of blood to that of skin. She lives on the streets, living off what she can steal. At night, she tells herself stories to keep the ghosts away.

'I am a ghost,' I tell her. I pass my hand through the air above her back, I am afraid to touch her even with my ghostly hand. I wish I could perform a miracle for her.

In a lake in my forest I met a fish once who had known a salmon, so I tell Sara the tale of the salmon's wanderings across the big, bottomless sea, right over the edge of the world and through the ocean that we think is the night sky. The salmon said that what look like stars to us are really the twinkling scales of fish in the water.

Sara listens. When I have finished my tale she looks up. She looks right into my eyes. She can hear me. She can see me.

She raises her hand and puts it on my arm. I can feel it. She can touch me. Her hand is so warm.

We sit there in a pew in my church, and look at each other.

Bibliography

This list is by no means exhaustive. The books on it are good places to start for finding out more about the saints of Wales, about the times some of them lived in, and about the workings of legend, myth and history:

Baring-Gould, Rev Sabine, *The Lives of the British Saints*, Honourable Society of Cymmrodorion, London, 1907

Beddoe, Deirdre, *Welsh Convict Women*, Stewart Williams Publishers, Barry, 1979

Brouten, Bernadette, *Love between Women, Early Christian responses to female homoeroticism*, University of Chicago Press, Chicago 1996

Doble, G.H. (ed Simon Evans), *Lives of the Welsh Saints*, University of Wales Press, Cardiff, 1984

Rees, Rev. W. J., *Lives of the Cambro British Saints*, Society for the Publication of Ancient Welsh Manuscripts, Abergavenny, 1853

Rees, Rice, B.D., *An Essay on the Welsh Saints or the Primitive Christians*, London, 1836.

Spencer, Ray, *A Guide to the Saints of Wales and the West Country*, Llanerch Press, Felinfach, 1901

Warner, Marina, *From the Beast to the Blonde*, Vintage, London, 1995

Ellen Galford's novel *The Fires of Bride* first gave me the idea to write this collection of stories.

Cofen was inspired by Alifa Rifaat's short story 'My World of the Unknown' (in *Distant View of a Minaret*, Heinemann, London, 1987)

Acknowledgements

Elke, Britta, Jane and Rachel for listening.

Magnetic North Writers' Group for feedback, support, challenges and suggestions.

Chris, who believed in me.

Lesley, Meena, Alexa, Donna, Frank, Sandra, Sue, Rosy and Vanina for encouragement and friendship.

All at Seren, for giving me a chance; and Penny Thomas in particular, for being a great editor to work with.

About the Author

Imogen Rhia Herrad is a freelance writer and broadcaster. Born and brought up in Germany, she has also lived in Wales (where she learnt Welsh) and in Argentina, and currently divides her time between London and Berlin.

Her short stories and articles have been published in magazines and anthologies in Wales, Canada and the United States.

Imogen won third prize in the London Writers' Competition for her children's story *The Wind's Bride*. Her short story *The Accident* was shortlisted in the Quality Women's Fiction 10th Anniversary Competition and longlisted for the Raymond Carver Short Story Awards.

The Woman who Loved an Octopus and other Saints' Tales is her first collection.

Maria Donovan

Pumping Up Napoleon ·-

and other Stories

Pumping Up Napoleon and other Stories is an assured collection of short stories with an offbeat take on human relationships, and the relationship of the rather unreliable body to mind and spirit.

'Offbeat' includes dog massage, cloning your own four-foot son for organ transplants and a university lecturer's romance with a resurrected Napoleon Bonaparte.

Maria Donovan takes us on a funny, bizarre and often touching tour of death and laughter, love and space travel. Her light, humorous touch allows darker strands to surface repeatedly – dislocated lives out of sync with their surroundings are set alongside human oddity and tenderness. These understated, well-crafted stories constantly surprise and engage, producing a fine enjoyable and thought-provoking first collection.

'These stories are remarkable, and engrossing: sometimes funny, sometimes sinister, always accomplished. Some will be classics.'

Fay Weldon

Seren £6.99
ISBN 978-1-85411-441-9
www. seren-books.com

Mr
CASSINI

Lloyd Jones

Longlisted for the Wales Book of the Year 2007

Mr Cassini is an amazing journey throught the geography of
one man's troubled mind as he tries to recover the lost years of
his childhood.

Duxie is a dreamer with holes in his memory. With the help
of the mysterious and beautiful Olly, he sets out on a quest to
fill the gaps. As they search the landscapes and myths of the
past, they uncover domestic and national tyranny.

The tale twists together strands of dream, daydream and
reality as Duxie journeys towards freedom – and an understanding of his amnesia. Lurking deep within his dreams is the
vampire-like Mr Cassini, who feeds off women's tears, keeps
stolen mannequins in a darkened room and commits terrible
acts with his policeman side-kick. Journeying through time,
Duxie investigates caves and sacred wells, mystics and
madness, and recruits four extraordinary champions for a
showcase trial on a mountain in the centre of Wales.

Seren £7.99

ISBN 1-85411-425-5

www.seren-books.com

Learning Resources
Centre